CLARA'S WAR

5.8/7.0

Clara's War

by

KATHY KACER

Second
Story
Press

National Library of Canada Cataloguing in Publication Data

Kacer, Kathy, 1954–
Clara's war

(A Holocaust remembrance book for young readers)
ISBN 1-896764-42-8

1. Theresienstadt (Concentration camp) — Juvenile fiction.
2. Jewish children in the Holocaust — Juvenile fiction.
3. Krása, Hans, 1899–1944. Brundibár — Juvenile fiction.
4. Jewish ghettos — Czechoslovakia — Juvenile fiction.
I. Title. II. Series: Holocaust remembrance book for young readers.

PS8571.A33C52 2001   jC813'.54   C2001-930269-X
PZ7.K32C1 2001

Edited by Sarah Silberstein Swartz
Copy edited by Terra Page
Cover illustration by Liz Milkau
Cover design by Stephanie Martin

*Second Story Press gratefully acknowledges the assistance of the
Ontario Arts Council and the Canada Council for the Arts
for our publishing program. We acknowledge the financial
support of the Government of Canada through the
Book Publishing Industry Development Program (BPIDP)
for our publishing activities.*

Photos on pages 191, 195, 196 reproduced with permission from the
Jewish Museum in Prague.

Artwork on page 192 reproduced with permission from
Wallstein Verlag GmbH.

Printed and bound in Canada

Published by
SECOND STORY PRESS
720 Bathurst Street, Suite 301
Toronto, Canada M5S 2R4
www.secondstorypress.on.ca

DEDICATION

In memory of my late father, Arthur Kacer
— a proud, gentle and hopeful man.

For my children, Gabi and Jake
— may they contribute to a world that is loving and peaceful.

ACKNOWLEDGEMENTS

This book would not have been possible without the help of John Freund, himself a survivor of Terezin and subsequently Auschwitz. He graciously read numerous versions of this book, helping ensure an authentic historical context. He shared with me countless stories about his life in Terezin as well as photographs and books. He has dedicated his life to promoting the memory of Terezin and to helping keep the opera "Brundibar" alive. It is a privilege to call him my friend.

Thanks also to Helena Fine and Sheila Koffman for reading the manuscript and contributing their feedback.

I have drawn information about Terezin from other sources including the books, *We Are Children Just the Same: Vedem, The Secret Magazine by the Boys of Terezin*, edited by Paul Wilson; and *Theresienstadt: The Town the Nazis Gave to the Jews*, by Vera Schiff. These books provided valuable information about day-to-day life in the ghetto.

I am indebted to Margie Wolfe of Second Story Press for her continued support of my writing, and to Terra Page for her diligence in the production of this book.

My warmest thanks to Sarah Silberstein Swartz for her invaluable editorial feedback, as well as her personal encouragement and guidance.

I am forever grateful for the love and support of my husband and children, Ian Epstein, Gabi and Jake. Their enthusiasm and faith in my writing are a continuous source of inspiration.

Preface

IN 1780, EMPEROR JOSEPH II built a fortress that he named after his mother, Maria Theresa. It lay in a town in the mountains of Bohemia (later called Czechoslovakia, and today the Czech Republic), northwest of Prague. The Czechs named the town "Terezin." The fortress had been built to protect Prague from invaders to the north. However in 1939, shortly after the start of World War II, German troops invaded the western part of Czechoslovakia and the land, including Terezin, became part of German-occupied territory.

In October 1941, Terezin became "Theresienstadt," a concentration camp that the Nazis called a "ghetto" for Jews. Its purpose was to temporarily house Jews before sending them on to Auschwitz and other death camps. Terezin was isolated from the rest of the country and could be easily guarded. It was therefore an ideal place to imprison Jews. The world was led to believe that Terezin had been a "gift" from Hitler to the Jews, a place where conditions were generally good and where Jews were being kept safe from the hardships of war. The Nazis created an elaborate propaganda campaign to divert attention away from their systematic murder of the Jewish people. The deception worked. While there are conflicting reports as to the exact numbers of people taken to Terezin, it is estimated that over 97,000 Czech Jews who were there died or were eventually deported east to other labour and death camps. Of that number, 15,000 were children. Only 132 children were known to have survived. The conditions in Terezin were appalling.

Inmates lived with hunger, disease, extreme overcrowding,

filth and the constant threat of deportations east to the death camps. Rules, which were issued on a daily basis, restricted the lives of the inmates. Men and women were separated. Children were kept apart from their parents. Contact between adults was forbidden. Letter writing was banned. Inmates could be beaten, hanged or deported for failure to observe these and many other rules.

The ghetto was run on a day-to-day basis by the Council of Jewish Elders, a committee of Jews appointed by the Nazis. They organized the work details, the food kitchens, the health facilities and the living quarters. They also had the terrible task of selecting those Jews who would be deported east, in order to make room for new Jews arriving in the ghetto on an almost daily basis. The Council was controlled by Czech guards who patrolled the ghetto. The ultimate authority in the camp was the Nazi commander and his troops. Though the Nazis only showed up periodically in Terezin, they were feared by all.

In the midst of these threatening conditions, some incredible events occurred. Music, art, theatre and other cultural performances took place in Terezin, inspired by a number of gifted musicians, artists, and other prominent individuals who were prisoners there. The Nazis allowed these cultural events to take place because it was one more way of distracting the Jews from focussing on their probable fate. The activities gave the inmates some false hope for survival. In addition, the Nazis actually enjoyed the cultural presentations and came to view them.

This is the setting for *Clara's War*, a place of fear and constant uncertainty for the young people of this time. But out of this tragedy came faith and courage. *Clara's War* brings together the horror and the hope that was the reality of Terezin.

Chapter One

LEAVING HOME

CLARA GRABBED her brother's arm and pulled him along the street, knowing the walk home from the centre of the city could be dangerous.

"Come on, Peter. You've got to walk faster." It seemed to Clara that she always had the job of looking after her younger brother. Mostly she didn't mind. But at times like this, when Peter dawdled, she hated every moment. It was bad enough that her parents had sent Peter with her to get the new coupons for their food. The lines at the government building on the main street of Prague were so long, and you had to be quick to get to the front. There was always the danger that soldiers or local bullies might appear, looking to stir up trouble. A group of Jewish people lined up for documents was just what they were after.

"It's better if you go as a pair," papa had said. "That way you can look out for each other." Clara knew that meant she had to look out for Peter. For the hundredth time, Clara reached into her pocket to make sure the food coupons were still there, and pulled one out to look at it. These were a lifeline for her family, more precious these days than almost anything else. The coupon was stamped with today's date, March 12, 1943. The coupons would last for about two weeks and then Clara would have to go out and line up again. Maybe next time, she'd sneak out without Peter.

"Peter, if you don't move faster, I'm going to leave you here and the Nazi guards will find you and arrest you." Whom was she kidding? There was no way that Clara was going to leave her eleven-year-old brother in the streets of Prague.

Peter kept his head down as he dragged his feet along, and Clara glared at him in frustration. He was small for his age, thin and bony with big green eyes that often looked uncertain and even unhappy. Peter had always been such a quiet boy, not at all like Clara who, at thirteen, was never at a loss for words. Clara's parents always marveled at how different their two children were. Clara was so curious and lighthearted, Peter so serious and withdrawn. Even their appearances were strikingly different, as if they had come from two different families. Peter was pale and blond, while Clara's brown curls matched her dark, lively eyes. And then there was Peter's temper. It flared when no one expected it and disappeared just as quickly. Peter was "complicated." That's how the family described him.

"If we took a little of you and a little of Peter, think what a perfect child we'd have," papa would sometimes joke. Clara didn't mind the teasing. She liked being the way she was, so outspoken and straightforward about everything. She didn't like being serious and quiet. Leave that to Peter, she thought, grabbing him by the arm and pulling him along the street.

Clara had walked this route to and from the centre of town hundreds, no maybe thousands of times. She knew each building without even having to look up. First there was the public school at the corner of the street. More than three years had passed since Clara and the other Jewish children had been forbidden to attend public school in Prague — three years since she was no longer allowed to socialize with her Christian friends. And while she still got to see her Jewish friends at the Jewish school she now attended, Clara wondered how long that would last. Her old public school friends were probably studying mathematics right now, or maybe history, thought Clara. From a window on the second floor came the sounds of the string orchestra tuning up, practising for a school assembly or an upcoming show. On the field, a group of students were running laps as part of their gym class.

Past the school was the synagogue, deserted now but once the thriving centre of her family's religious life. Now the door was boarded up, and on the front wall someone had painted the words OUT JEWS in capital letters. Next to the synagogue was the park. How often had Clara slipped out of Saturday morning services so she and her friends could walk in the park? There stood the biggest oak tree, whose trunk was split at the bottom. Every year, Clara's parents had taken pictures of her and Peter sitting in that tree. They often said that it was a spot just begging for photographs to be taken. The collection of pictures in the family album was like a record of how they had grown and changed over the years. Today the park was closed to all Jews.

Even the shops, once so familiar and inviting, now only depressed Clara as she walked by. Mrs. Klein's bakery, where Clara and her friends had bought sugar donuts at least once a week, was now closed. So was the butcher shop, which had belonged to Mr. Kaufman, where all the Jewish families had bought their kosher meat, prepared according to Jewish law. Nazi rules restricting Jews from owning any businesses had forced these shopkeepers to close their stores. Besides, what good was a store if no one bought anything from you? The other shops, the flower shop, the candy store, the clothier, were still open, but the sign on their doors was unmistakable: NO JEWS ALLOWED!

Clara missed the candy store most of all. Mrs. Shebek used to hand out sweets to all the children walking to school. "Sweets for my sweeties," she would say. Lately she wouldn't even look at Clara when she walked by.

Life had changed dramatically for her family and all the Jews living in Prague, since the Nazi army had occupied her city on March 15, 1939. There was a time when walking down the street had been fun and going to the centre of town an adventure. But that time seemed so long ago. It was four years since the Munich Agreement had been signed, turning over the western part of Czechoslovakia to Germany and its ruling Nazi Party, lead by Adolf Hitler. Despite the agreement, war in Europe had begun in 1939, when Germany invaded Poland to the north and east of Czechoslovakia. Hitler was a heartless and brutal leader who hated Jews and wanted them punished for everything bad that had ever happened to the German people. Jews were being falsely blamed for businesses doing poorly, for poverty and for the lack of jobs. Since the invasion of Poland, the rules and restrictions against Jews in all Nazi-occupied lands had multiplied on an almost daily basis.

Clara's father, a respected doctor, had been dismissed from his post at the nearby hospital at about the same time Clara had stopped going to public school. Luckily for now, papa could still work at the Jewish clinic. Clara and the others wore yellow badges shaped in a Star of David to identify them as Jews. Once you wore the star, Christian neighbours like Mrs. Novak stopped talking to you. They feared for their own safety. Just last week Clara had witnessed Mr. Novak helping an old Jewish man who was being bullied by a group of young hoodlums. The police arrived and arrested both Mr. Novak and the old Jew. Important Jewish leaders were regularly arrested and taken away. No one knew where they were taken. Jewish households were ordered to hand over their possessions, such as furs, jewellery, textiles and silverware, to the authorities. Each time one of these new laws appeared Clara would brace herself thinking, surely this is the last one. Her parents always tried to assure her that it couldn't possibly get any worse. But each time it did get worse.

"Just one more block and then we'll be home," said Clara as she instinctively put an arm around her brother. He shrugged her off and sprinted for home. *Now* he's running, thought Clara as she took off in pursuit of Peter. Around the corner they ran, competing now to be the first into their apartment building. He may be small, thought Clara, but when he wants to be, he certainly is fast! Peter swung the big iron door open and took the stairs two at a time with Clara just behind.

The moment Clara entered the apartment, she knew there was trouble. Her parents stood silently in the living room next to the front door. Together they stared in silence at the single sheet of paper in papa's hands.

"What is it, papa?" asked Clara anxiously. "What's wrong?"

Mama looked alarmed. She opened her mouth to speak but no words came out. Instead, helplessly, she lowered her eyes to avoid looking at her children. It was left to papa to deliver the news.

"It's a notice — a new rule," stammered papa. "We've been ordered to leave here."

"You mean we're going on a trip?" Peter spoke for the first time. His large round eyes bulged and he chewed nervously on the sleeve of his shirt, an old childhood habit.

"If you mean a holiday, then I'm afraid the answer is no, Peter." Papa swallowed hard as he looked at his children. "We've been ordered to leave our home. We're being taken to live someplace else." A sharp gasp escaped from Peter, while Clara tried to understand what she was hearing. How could this be true?

"Where are we going, papa?" Clara asked.

"Sixty kilometres north and west of Prague. The Nazis have set aside a place for the Jews of Prague and other cities. It is a small town surrounded by a wall where we Jews will live apart from everyone else. They call it a 'ghetto.' The letter says we'll have a home there and we'll live a normal life. The town is called Terezin."

Terezin. Clara let the word roll around on her tongue. Vaguely she recalled the name from her history class, the town with the fortress built by Emperor Joseph II of Austria over two hundred years ago. She remembered that the fortress had been built to protect Prague from invaders. Now her family was being ordered to leave their home for this strange town.

"When do we have to leave, papa?" asked Peter, so quietly Clara had to strain to hear him.

"March 14, 1943. Two days from now," mama replied, as if she had memorized the date on the notice. She looked around the apartment in desperation. "What to pack first?" Her eyes moved from the paintings on the wall, each one lovingly chosen, to the porcelain statue on the mantle above the fireplace, a gift at her own wedding. "What will we take with us?" she asked as her eyes rested on the large bookshelf in the front room. Mama, a former librarian, loved to read and over the years had accumulated an extensive collection of rare books that she loved dearly.

"Not much I'm afraid, mama," replied papa. "We're only allowed four pieces of luggage, fifty kilograms in total."

"And what will we leave behind?" Tears gathered in mama's eyes.

Everything, thought Clara. Home, friends, family members, neighbours, clothing, personal keepsakes. All she had ever known. All that was secure and familiar. Clara turned as Peter ran for his bedroom, slamming the door hard behind him. From behind the door, they could all hear his angry, muffled cries.

"Come, mama, Clara," said papa, removing his glasses to wipe his own eyes. "We have much to do."

Chapter Two

MOVING DAY

"CLARA, FOR THE THIRD TIME, wake up! It's 3:00 a.m. and you know we have to be at the train station soon." Clara's mother bent once more to shake her daughter, frustrated by her refusal to move.

"Five more minutes," Clara moaned from beneath her covers. "I promise I'll get up if you just give me five more minutes."

From deep inside the warmth and darkness of her room, Clara had been lost in the most wonderful dream and she didn't want it to end. She had been flying like a bird above her beloved Prague, looking down on its beautiful buildings, statues and parks. Below her the rush of water from the Moldau River flowed quickly toward the Charles Bridge. There, hundreds of people strolled, stopping periodically to watch artists paint scenes of the Prague Castle, or listen to street musicians playing for small change. Flowers were in bloom along the banks of the river and Clara's flight led her through winding cobblestone streets, underneath court-yard archways and past the statue of Saint Wenceslas in the square. It was like noticing the beauty of her city for the first time, and Clara felt free. Coming out of her dream, she was yanked back to earth and reality with a thud.

"Clara, get up now!" mama called once more and with a heavy sigh Clara rolled out of bed to her last morning in her home. Her suitcase was already packed. There was nothing more to do than get washed, dressed and eat something before leaving.

Clara looked at the pile of clothing on the chair and started putting on three pairs of underwear, two sets of stockings, two skirts, two blouses, three sweaters and a dress. It was mama's way of "packing" extra clothes beyond the limit the family was allowed.

Clara finished dressing and looked in the mirror, trying unsuccessfully to smooth down her long, unmanageable dark curls. She hated the curls. Why couldn't her hair be straight like her mother's, or at least blond like Peter's? Her brown eyes flashed as she looked at herself carefully in the mirror. Whom would she meet in this new place, she wondered. Clara was already familiar with Jews being ordered to leave Prague. She had watched many friends and family members leave their homes with similar notices in their hands. Still, somehow Clara had believed it would never happen to her family. Her father's position as a doctor had provided some protection for them in the midst of the war. Doctors were still needed in Prague, even the ones who only took care of Jewish people.

"This is ridiculous," Clara said aloud, as she finished

dressing. "I look like I've gained five kilos."

"It's important," mama reminded Clara as she joined her family at the table to eat their last meal together in their flat. "We don't know how long we'll be there. And we need to take as much clothing as we can." She urged Clara to eat one more roll with cheese and to finish drinking her hot cup of tea.

Mama's voice was firm, but her eyes looked tired and sad. In the last two days, mama had walked around in a daze. Clara would catch her standing in front of an old family picture, lost in the memory of an earlier time. Mama and papa had lived in this apartment since the day they married and losing it was like losing a member of the family.

"Peter," said papa. "Have you finished packing your things?" Peter nodded quietly, looking even more gloomy than he normally did.

"Do you think I can take my soccer ball, papa?" he asked. Peter lived for soccer. It was the one activity that made him come alive. His surprising speed had made him a secret weapon for his school. Even after he and Clara had been expelled from school, Peter practised soccer in the courtyard outside their building every day. Neighbours often complained about the sound of the ball slamming against the wall and nearly missing windows.

"No, my son, I think the ball will have to stay here. There are more important things we must bring. But perhaps there will be soccer in Terezin," he added.

By 3:30 a.m. Clara, her parents and Peter were all

moving quickly in the apartment, grabbing last minute belongings and stuffing them into their suitcases. They tried to make final decisions about this keepsake or that personal memento, weighing its importance against one more practical thing. After the packing was finished, mama straightened up the flat as if preparing it for visitors.

"Why bother, mama?" Clara asked. "We don't even know what's going to happen to the apartment once we leave." Mama was forever tidying.

"I want to leave our home looking perfect. That way, I'll always remember how beautiful it is," she replied.

Clara's father gathered the suitcases and took them to the front hall. Clara came back to take one last look at her bedroom. Her eyes scanned the room, resting briefly on every object, straining to memorize each detail — her white, four-poster bed and matching dresser and desk, the doll-house in the corner complete with its tiny, hand-carved wooden furniture, the flowered wallpaper she had watched her father put up on her eighth birthday. Clara took deep breaths, as if to capture the smells she knew so well and add them to her memories. If I don't come back for a while, I don't want to forget any of this, she thought. Finally, she closed the door and joined her family in the living room.

The last thing papa did was to drop the key to their flat on the dining room table. Suddenly what had been theirs no longer belonged to them. Tears glistened in mama's eyes, as papa reassuringly placed his arm around her. "Come, mama, we must go."

Mama stood in front of the small cabinet next to the front door, stroking its surface. "Just one more minute. I ... I need to stay just one more minute," whispered mama as the tears finally spilled over and streamed down her cheeks. "I didn't think it would be like this — so painful, so fast." Mama looked small and defeated.

"We must look forward now, mama." Papa held himself tall and proud.

Peter buried his head deep in his overcoat as Clara clutched her father's hand. Don't look back, she thought, trying to listen to papa's strong words. Look ahead.

Clara and her family walked the two kilometres to the train station, past her school, the synagogue and the park. How long would it be before she saw those sites again, she wondered. They arrived at the station so early the sky was still dark and the morning looked like night. There was a cool wind, blowing the branches of the trees in all directions as if waving goodbye. Farewell Prague, Clara thought.

The summons informing them that they were being transported away had said to be at the station at 5:00 a.m. "Better to be early," papa said with his usual wisdom. "Who knows how many others have received a summons? This way we will be sure to get seats on the train. We don't want to be uncomfortable for the trip."

I'm already uncomfortable, Clara thought, sweating beneath the layers of clothing. They got to the station at 4:00 a.m. But they were not the only ones there early. Hundreds of people lined the streets in front of the depot, each family pushing to get as close to the front as possible. Clara wanted to be at the back. Maybe that way, she wouldn't have to go.

"Do you think there will be room for everyone on the train?" asked Clara. No one answered. In the past two days, her parents had stopped answering many of her questions.

"Why do we have to go?" she had asked repeatedly.

"Because the authorities say we must," was the reply.

"But why?"

"Because that's the new law."

"But what if we refuse to go?"

"We can't refuse."

"But why?" No answer.

Clara's family finally made it to the front of the line. There, at a small desk, sat a dour-looking German official.

"Identity cards," he snapped. Papa quickly turned over the little booklets with their photographs and the capital letter "J" identifying them as Jews. Their names were clearly written on the front; Simon and Helen Berg, and their children, Clara Berg and Peter Berg. In the place of these papers, papa received cards, each with a number, and handed them to his family to hang around their necks. It was as if their names, like their home, were being taken away. They would no longer need papers to identify themselves. What did this mean?

When their numbers were called, everyone hurried to gather their cases and proceed to the platform. German officers barked orders at them as they boarded the train and scrambled to find seats. Papa pushed ahead, finally managing to find four seats together in one corner of the train. Others were not so lucky and had to stand in the aisles, jammed together like Clara's dolls at home when she shoved them into the back of her cupboard. Everyone looked lost and terrified.

A small girl sobbed on her mother's shoulder. "I don't want to go on the train, mama. I want to go home," she cried.

"Shhhh. There, there, my sweet child. Put your head here on my shoulder and sleep now." The mother stroked her child's head and rocked her back and forth, whispering gently into her ear. She kissed her daughter's forehead as tears rolled down her own cheeks. Clara turned away. She too wanted to cry, but knew at her age she needed to be brave.

The train slowly left the station, moving west toward the town that would be their new home. It was filled with frightened families, all wondering what life would hold for them in the next days and months. Papa's face looked remarkably calm. But papa always looked calm and Clara relied on his unruffled strength to bolster her own. Mama's face, on the other hand, betrayed her fears. Peter dozed off as the sound of the engine rocked many to sleep with its steady rhythm.

Where are we going? a little voice inside Clara's head screamed. What will we find there? Will we be safe? Will we ever come back home? The other rules and laws had changed everything about her life. But this one was ripping away her life as she knew it. Clara closed her eyes and tried to recapture the dream she had had the night before. But it escaped her. Clara's dream, like her city of Prague, was quickly disappearing behind her.

Chapter Three

ARRIVING IN TEREZIN

THE TRAIN SLOWED down and then came to a sudden halt, jolting everyone awake.

"Huh? Where are we?" Peter asked, looking around. Through the window of the passenger train the sky was grey and a brown misty cloud hung low on the horizon.

In a matter of minutes, the doors opened and guards in uniform moved through the train, shouting orders to disembark. "Everyone off the train. Move quickly. Take all your belongings. Move! Move!"

Everyone scrambled to gather cases and shuffled briskly toward the opening. Papa turned to help mama off, while Peter and Clara jumped to the ground and looked around. The sign in the station read "Bohusovice." From the map of the country that had been in papa's study at home, Clara knew this place was the closest station to Terezin, approximately three kilometres from the city. Around her, there was bedlam. Guards shouted commands, small children cried, people shoved and pushed. Clara wanted to look around her but was afraid she would lose sight of her family.

"Leave your cases on the platform. They will be transported by wagon. Form a line. Follow the officers at the front. Stop talking. Move! Move!" The orders continued, fast and furious. Where was Peter? Where was her mother? Suddenly, a small figure grabbed Clara from behind and whirled her around.

"Clara! You're here, too?" Clara couldn't believe someone knew her name. Dazed for a moment, she stared at her friend, Hanna Klein.

"Hanna? Oh Hanna, I'm so glad to see someone I know. Is your whole family with you?"

"Yes, they're back there, helping my grandparents off the train. Do you believe this place? All those guards with their guns scare me." Clara nodded in agreement. Why on earth were there so many guards? wondered Clara. Did they actually believe anyone would have the courage to escape from the crowd and run?

"Move ahead! Stop talking!" Once more the guards bellowed at the passengers.

"Try to look for me whenever we get to where we're going," Hanna whispered, after giving Clara a quick hug. Clara turned again to search for her family and saw her mother anxiously inspecting the crowd.

"Clara," mama cried, relieved to have spotted her daughter. "Don't leave us. We must stay together. Hold my hand and don't let go of me." Mama grabbed Clara's arm and together they pushed through the crowd until they spied the rest of the family up ahead.

The crowd was forced into lines, surrounded on all sides by guards holding rifles. They moved forward in a slow march toward the town. We must be a pitiful sight, thought Clara — hundreds and hundreds of exhausted and frightened people, heads bent, walking cautiously through the fog. Old men and women stumbled in the dirt as the guards continued shouting orders. Dogs with big, ugly teeth snarled and snapped as the guards let them move out on their leashes and then yanked them back just before they could reach the people. Children cried as their weary parents tried to hush them. A sense of fearful expectation hung in the air.

It took almost an hour by foot to reach the outskirts of Terezin and to cross over the moat into the old town. It was isolated and easy to guard because of the high-reaching walls. The first stop was a large warehouse where each person was given new ration cards. Clara and her family reclaimed their luggage at the next stop and proceeded to the inspection area. The jars of preserves mama had stored in the bottom of her suitcase were quickly confiscated, along with their toothpaste, soap and the one precious book mama had brought along. These items were not allowed, they were told.

There was so much commotion around her, Clara could barely take a breath before being pushed on to each new stop. There was no time to pause and take in her surroundings — no time for anything but to keep up with the movement of the crowd. Guards were everywhere, maintaining order while keeping the tired and frightened people moving.

Finally, it was time to grab their bags once more and find out where they were going to be living. The last command was the most alarming of all.

"Men's barracks to the left, women to the right. Children, straight ahead."

Surely this was a mistake! Clara looked quickly at her parents. They looked as shocked as she felt.

"Mama, we're not going to be together," Clara gasped, grabbing her mother's arm in terror as the crowd surged forward.

There was no time to say goodbye before the line divided into the three designated groups. Clara's head pounded with fear and Peter's round eyes bulged as he turned, desperately searching out mama and papa in the crowd. Help me, his eyes pleaded. Don't let them take me away from you! The sound of children crying for their parents swelled as Clara scanned the crowd, finally locking on to her parents' faces.

"Clara," papa called. "Try to stay with Peter. We will look for you as soon as we can."

Mama couldn't speak, but raised her arm to wave and then Clara and her brother were once again swept forward. Her throat tightened. Not even the sight of papa, so strong and tall, could reassure her. All around, young children were crying, and being comforted by others only a few years older. Clara hung tightly on to Peter's hand.

"Are these two bags yours?" A young boy stood in front of her, pointing down at the suitcases. Clara nodded, still unable to say a word.

"Okay, I'll take this one, and you two grab the other one. I'm Jacob Langer and I'll help you find your building." Jacob bent forward to lift the bigger of the two suitcases as Clara paused to look at him. The boy who called himself Jacob was very thin and looked about fifteen years old. His clothes were shabby, threadbare and torn, and too small on his tall body. Clara couldn't help noticing how he tugged awkwardly at his shirt sleeves as if pulling at them might make them longer. And yet, there was something interesting about him. He looked like someone who knew his way around.

"My name is Clara Berg and this is my brother, Peter," said Clara, as the three of them moved forward.

Jacob curiously eyed the two new arrivals. The boy looked frightened and delicate, he thought. The girl looked strong and smart. That was good. She would need it here.

"Okay, Clara and Peter, this is the way it works," said Jacob in a confident voice as they walked. "These two buildings here in the centre of town are the dormitories for kids under sixteen years of age, one for girls and one for boys. Peter, you're in this building up ahead. It's also my building, but you'll be with boys your own age. I'll introduce you to the others once you're settled. Clara, you're in the girls' dormitory right here, not so far away from your brother. The rooms may not look like much, but trust me, they're a lot better that the ones the grown-ups get." Clara winced, wondering where mama and papa were at that moment.

"Try to take a bunk on the top," continued Jacob.

"You'll get extra breathing space and some privacy up there. If there's anything you need to know, just ask. It takes a while to learn the rules. I can help you figure some things out. As long as you stay here things will be okay. You just don't want to be sent away from here."

Why? Clara wondered. What happens to those who leave? There was no time to ask questions. Instead she looked around for the first time since arriving.

Surrounding her were three-storey brick buildings, not unlike her apartment building at home, but dirtier and run-down. Farther back were other, smaller buildings partially blocked from view by the larger structures in front. Here and there, through the doorways and windows of buildings, Clara caught a glimpse of grown-ups crammed together in dirty, crowded barracks, lying on torn mattresses and small cots. Was this how she was also going to live? Clara shuddered.

In the centre of the town, they passed a large town square, fenced in and clearly off-limits. The square was the size of a park, but barren, muddy and deserted. Not one blade of grass, one tree or one flower was to be seen anywhere in this gloomy place. In fact, there was no colour anywhere in Terezin. It was as if the reds and blues and yellows and greens of the real world had been washed away. In their place, everything was grey and brown and dull.

An old man leaning heavily on a wooden stick pushed past, knocking Peter so hard he almost fell over. Peter's eyes flashed with anger and for a moment Clara thought he might go after the man. But the moment passed and Peter hung his head once more, chewing nervously on his sleeve. Thousands of people seemed to be walking through the streets of Terezin. It was hard at times to keep up with Jacob and not lose him in the crowd. How many people were crammed inside these few buildings? Clara thought.

As if reading her mind, Jacob turned to talk over his shoulder. "There are over 40,000 Jews in Terezin right now. Sometimes I'm not sure how we all fit in this place."

The streets and sidewalks were narrow and at practically every cross street stood several guards. The guards looked alert, rifles pointed forward, eyes glued on the inmates moving wearily through the streets. The expressions on their faces were frightening. They seemed to be waiting for a confrontation so they could prove who was in charge.

"Watch out for that guard," Jacob warned, pointing toward a man in uniform with a deep scowl on his face. "His name is Heindl. Most of the Czech guards are okay. But he's a Nazi. He's trouble and it's best to stay out of his way." Clara was about to ask what he meant, when Jacob interrupted her thoughts.

"Okay, Clara, this is as far as I can go. You'll be able to see Peter when we line up for food. Don't worry. I'll watch out for him."

Clara took her case and turned to face her brother. Peter had not spoken a word from the time they had arrived at the train station in Bohusovice, but the fear in his eyes was unmistakable.

"Peter, I'll see you soon. I promise." Clara tried to make her voice sound as strong and confident as she could, though she felt neither. She hugged her brother quickly and watched as he and Jacob moved toward their building. Peter's head hung low and his shoulders slumped forward meekly. Clara wanted to run after him, as much for her sake as his. She felt more alone than she had ever felt in her life. She gulped back her tears, turned and walked up the steps to what was to become her new home.

Chapter Four

THE GIRLS' DORMITORY

CLARA ENTERED room number six at the top of the stairs. I have to get through this, she thought, as the tears finally rolled down her cheeks. I have no choice. More than ever, Clara needed her parents and she didn't even know where they were. Never before had she felt so alone. She stood at the door wondering what to do.

"Clara, I'm so glad to see you're here," a familiar voice called to her.

"Hanna!" Clara cried, hugging her friend fiercely and wiping her tear-stained cheeks. "Are you supposed to be in this room too?" When Hanna nodded, Clara grabbed her again. "Oh, you don't know how happy that makes me!"

The two girls stood for several seconds clutching each other. Hanna was like a piece of home for Clara. The two girls had been good friends in Prague. Many times, Hanna had gone out of her way to help Clara. One time, Clara had been sick with the flu for a week. Without being asked, Hanna had brought schoolwork home for her every day. In the midst of all that was unfamiliar and frightening in

Terezin, Clara had a close friend!

Finally, the two girls stepped apart to examine their room. The room was faintly lit by a single light bulb, hanging from the centre of the ceiling. The bunk beds were three levels high with ladders for climbing at each end. Clara could see from the number of beds pushed together that the room held about thirty people, though at the moment it was empty. A long wooden table with benches ran through the middle of the room. And that was it.

"Pretty awful, isn't it?" Clara said, shuddering at the bare room's coldness.

Hanna nodded. "Do you think we should go in?"

Clara remembered Jacob's advice about the top bunk and suggested to Hanna that they find a place to put their things.

The girls picked up their cases and entered the room, checking each bed carefully to see if any appeared to be vacant. Most of the beds were occupied. Jackets, shirts and socks were strewn about. The walls of several bunks were covered in messages, scratched into the wooden wall with a nail or knife. Clara bent closer to get a better look. There were carved names and dates, presumably of previous occupants. Where had they gone? wondered Clara, remembering the reference Jacob had made to those who leave the ghetto. She stood up and strained her neck to get a look at the top bunks and finally spotted one that looked empty.

"There, Hanna," she said. "I'm going to climb up there to see if anyone's using that bed." Clara moved to the foot of the cot and mounted the ladder. "There are two empty spots up here next to each other. Hand me the suitcases and I'll put them on the beds."

Clara was struggling to push the second case up the ladder when she heard footsteps on the stairs and the sound of children's voices. She scrambled down quickly, just as a group of about twenty-five girls, all about her age, burst through the door. They came to a complete stop when they saw Hanna and Clara. The girls were thin and pale, as if they had not eaten well in a long time. It frightened Clara to see a group of girls her age looking so sickly. Their clothes were shabby, from having been worn a little too often and not cleaned enough. They stared curiously at Hanna and Clara. A young woman, about twenty years of age, pushed through the group to stand in front of them.

"So, you're the two new girls. Are you Clara?" she asked. Clara nodded. "Good, then you must be Hanna. I'm sorry we weren't here to greet you. We had permission to go outside, so we've been in the courtyard. We didn't expect that you'd arrive so early. My name is Marta Adler and I'm the leader in this room."

Marta was warm and kind looking, a beautiful young woman even in the midst of the misery of the ghetto. She reminded Clara of Mrs. Slaba, one of her favourite teachers from her old school. Marta extended her hands to Hanna and Clara and maneuvered them throughout the group of girls, stopping periodically to introduce several of them. One by one, the girls said their names and welcomed Clara and Hanna to their new home. It sounded strange to Clara's ears to hear everyone call this place a home. She couldn't help wondering if she would ever come to think of it that way.

"I see that you've already selected your bunks," Marta continued. "Good for you. Why don't you unpack your things and we'll move the cases out of the way. The other girls need to tidy up their cots before we go to eat," she said, glancing meaningfully at the group. "Ask me or the others any questions you have. We're here to help you get settled." With that, she moved down the room to a lower bunk that was hers. The other girls surrounded Clara and Hanna, staring inquiringly.

"Where are you from?" one blond-haired girl asked. "I'm from Brno," she said, naming a city to the east.

"We're both from Prague," Clara replied. "What were you doing outside?" She couldn't imagine that anything interesting could happen here.

"We were playing volleyball," another girl said. "We try to get permission to go into the courtyard every afternoon to get some exercise. We'd go crazy and make sure to drive Marta crazy, if we had to stay inside all day long." The girls laughed, glancing in Marta's direction.

There was laughter in this room and even some fun. It was all so confusing. One minute, Clara felt afraid and the next minute she felt calm. One moment things seemed awful, and the next, things felt hopeful. One minute she was being pulled away from her parents and brother, and the next, she was talking to girls her age who were playing ball. It was too much for Clara to understand.

She turned and climbed the ladder to her bunk to begin unpacking her bags. There was nothing but clothes left inside. Even the books she had stuffed in had been seized by the guards, along with her writing paper and pens. In a matter of minutes, she had finished unpacking, removed the extra layers of clothing and moved her case to the side of the wall. Curiously, she approached a number of girls to find out more about where they were from and what had happened to them since coming to Terezin. Sonia, a small girl with sad brown eyes who was from Berlin, Germany told Clara she had been here six months. She told Clara how lucky she was not to have come during the winter. The buildings had little heat and in the absence of warm winter clothing, many children had become sick.

"But that's not nearly as bad as the heat in summer," interrupted Erika, a tall pretty girl with dark brown hair. She had been in Terezin for ten months and had experienced both summer and winter. "In summer, it's so hot we can hardly breathe in here. But the biggest problem is the water. It's not very clean and there's not much of it. One day in the middle of the worst heat wave, the guards made us march around the square for hours with no shade and nothing to drink. I fainted and so did a bunch of the others. Winter seemed easy compared to that." The girls around her nodded in agreement.

One by one stories emerged of insufficient food, bad water, sickness, unbearable cold and heat. Clara felt her stomach churn. Hanna's face looked equally pale as she sat quietly listening to the girls' stories.

"But you know what?" said Sonia. "Anything's better than being transported away from here." The others nodded in agreement.

"Jacob, the boy I met when we arrived, said something about that as well." Clara spoke up. "What happens to people who leave here? Where do they go?"

The girls looked at one another cautiously and then Erika replied. "Well, we don't know too much about it, mostly rumours. But we do know that there are other camps east of here where things are much worse. So whatever happens, you don't want to get a note telling you to pack your things and report for re-location. That's what happened to Alice, the girl who used to be in your bed," she said, nodding in Hanna's direction. "And to others. We never heard from them again."

Silence hung in the air as the impact of Erika's words sunk in. Clara felt sick when she thought about the possibility of being sent away to someplace even worse than Terezin. Being here was bad enough. More than anything she needed to see her parents and brother, to know they were alright and to look in their eyes for a sign of reassurance. As if reading her mind, Marta approached the group.

"Come girls, it's time to line up outside the kitchen for food rations. Clara and Hanna, if we go quickly you may be lucky enough to see your families. Join the line, but be quiet. We must move quickly and orderly."

That was the cue Clara needed. Lining up promptly,

they all moved as a group, down the stairs and out the door. At the head of the line, Marta lead the girls through the streets of Terezin toward the kitchen, several buildings away. Around them other groups of children, varying in age, were also walking to get their suppers. The guards were everywhere, not necessarily interfering with the march, but just watching to make sure everyone moved along in an orderly fashion.

Clara anxiously inspected the crowd, searching for Peter, and finally found him to her left. Walking with his head down, he looked so small and lost. Look at me, Peter, Clara's eyes implored. Raise your head and look my way. Just then Clara spotted Jacob walking behind Peter. When Jacob saw her, he gently nudged Peter to look in her direction. Peter's face was numb, but his eyes brightened at the sight of his sister. Jacob gave Clara a quick thumbs up. With his hand reassuringly placed on Peter's shoulder, his group continued to move ahead.

Outside the kitchen, Clara's eyes desperately searched for her parents. She began to panic that she may have missed them when she suddenly spotted mama at the front of the food line, ladling what looked like very thin soup for each child. Clara caught her breath at the sight of her mother. Mama looked pale but otherwise fine. Clara wanted to run to the front of the line and throw herself into her mother's arms. But she knew it was impossible. Dozens of guards were everywhere, trying to maintain order, while the crowds of people kept pushing and shoving to get ahead. Everyone was desperate for food and the line moved with agonizing slowness. After what seemed like an eternity to Clara, she was finally at the front. Seeing her daughter standing before her, mama gasped sharply and fumbled with her wooden serving spoon.

"Clara! My sweet, darling child," she whispered, glancing nervously at the soldiers. "Are you alright? Where's Peter?"

"I'm okay, mama, and Peter is fine. I tried to stay with him, just like papa said, but I couldn't. Where's papa? Is he okay?" Clara sensed it was dangerous to talk, but she had to find out how her parents were. Knowing they were alright would give Clara some comfort. Mama slowly spooned the soup into Clara's metal plate.

"Your father has been assigned to the hospital and I'll be working here in the kitchen. I'm so lucky, Clara, that I got this job. I'll be able to see you at each meal and more often as time goes on. Here, take an extra roll," she said, slipping the bun onto Clara's plate and reaching up to gently brush her daughter's cheek with her hand.

"I miss you, mama." Tears gathered in Clara's eyes.

"Be strong, Clarichka," mama said, using her special nickname for Clara. "You and Peter are in my prayers."

Clara could delay no longer and the line pushed her ahead with her food while her stomach sank. She thought that seeing mama would help make her feel better. But it was not enough. She wanted more of her mother, and of her father and Peter.

Slowly the line returned to room six where Clara and the others ate their meal in silence. Then they washed their tin plates and cups in the cold bathroom water and prepared for bed. Closing her eyes, Clara tried to block out the events of the day, but that was impossible. So much had already happened and this was only day number one. It was hard to believe that just this morning Clara had awakened in the comfort of her own bed in her home with her parents and brother next door. Now she was lying on a cold hard cot in the middle of a strange place with only strangers around her. How am I ever going to manage being here? the voice inside Clara's head screamed. How am I ever going to be able to look out for Peter and look after myself? Clara was angry at the world for deserting her and terrified at being so alone.

Briefly, she thought about the girl who had previously occupied this bed and wondered where she was sleeping tonight. Was she feeling even more scared than Clara? Clara heard Hanna crying softly next to her and reached out to hold her hand. Back home, Hanna had been so cheery, a real chatterbox. Here in Terezin, numbed by the impact of the first day, Hanna had become oddly quiet. Only her bedtime tears spoke of what she was feeling and thinking.

At the other end of the room, one of the girls cried out as if in pain. Quickly Marta rose from her bed and rushed to the girl's cot, stroking her arm to calm her and stop her from waking others with her frightened sobs. All around the room, girls whimpered in their sleep, their voices creating an eerie melody. Clara was not the only one to miss her family. They were together in their sorrow and all alone at the same time. Exhaustion finally overcame Clara and she drifted to sleep.

Chapter Five

JACOB

NEARBY IN THE BOYS' DORMITORY, Jacob was also getting ready for bed and thinking about the transport that had arrived that day. He made a mental note to go and check on the new boy, Peter, before the lights went out. There was something about that boy that made Jacob feel he needed to offer help. Maybe it was that Peter was so unhappy and seemed so helpless. That was understandable, thought Jacob. After all, being torn away from your home and your parents all in one day was too much for any kid Peter's age. Or maybe it was that Peter's sister, Clara, seemed so worried about him. While Peter seemed so young, Clara seemed older and more mature than the other thirteen-year-old girls in Terezin. Whatever the reason, Jacob promised himself he would pay special attention to Peter. But first, he had to put away the new clothes he had found that day.

Jacob nodded his head in satisfaction as he folded the large shirt and sweater and tucked them into the small shelf next to his bed. He'd been lucky that day. In the new transport, he had managed to find a father with a young boy. In exchange for some of the man's clothes, Jacob had offered some of his own small clothes to the boy. The father had readily agreed, thinking that his son's warmth and comfort was worth some of his own. So now Jacob had some new clothes, not brand new, but at least big enough to fit. And not a moment too soon. These days, he seemed to outgrow his own clothes on an almost weekly basis.

Jacob moved toward the door. You had to be smart to survive in the ghetto, he thought. But then again, he had been surviving on his own long before his arrival in Terezin. Jacob was an orphan, his parents had been killed in an accident when he was still an infant. He had been raised in the orphanage in Prague and had been sent to Terezin six months earlier, along with many other Jewish orphans.

"I'm glad I found you. There's something you have to hear," said a nearby voice. Jacob looked up to see his friend Martin walking up the stairs with a pencil and notebook in his hand. Martin always carried paper with him wherever he went. He called himself a journalist and he was one of a group of boys who wrote articles for a secret magazine in the ghetto. They called the magazine "Vedem." It meant "In the Lead." A group of boys had started writing the magazine in 1942, painstakingly copying articles, poems and even jokes late at night, in the darkness of their barracks. A single copy of the magazine was "published" weekly and read aloud at house meetings. It was a vital part of the boys' lives in this dormitory.

"So what's in the news today, Martin," said Jacob, indicating the paper in Martin's hand. Having a constant supply of paper was difficult enough in the ghetto. But, somehow Martin and the others always managed to scrounge some up.

"I'm writing an article about the new transport," said Martin. "Do you want to hear some of it?"

Jacob nodded, all the time aware that the lights were going to go out shortly. He had to get to Peter, he thought again as Martin moved up to stand next to him on the stairs.

"*March 14, 1943*," began Martin, clearing his throat. "*Another transport of two thousand people arrived in Terezin today, a larger transport than usual. The inmates were from Prague and surrounding cities, as well as from Warsaw, Poland and Budapest. This brings to approximately 43,000 the number of Jews currently living in the ghetto. The readers may be aware that reports estimate at least 25,000 Jews have died or been sent east from Terezin in the past three years, but there are constantly new arrivals to take their place. So the ghetto is more crowded than ever.*

"*Today, the Council of Jewish Elders was on hand to greet the new arrivals,*" continued Martin. "*Jakob Edelstein, the Chairman of the Council welcomed the crowd and informed them that as long as they followed the rules of the ghetto, they would be fine. The group was orderly and quite calm. More reports will follow as these new inmates settle into their routines.*"

Martin paused to look up. "What do you think?"

Jacob didn't answer. His head was swimming with the information in Martin's report. Twenty-five thousand Jewish inmates had already died in Terezin or been sent away, thought Jacob in disbelief. While he knew that people were constantly dying or disappearing, it was hard to really comprehend how large the numbers were. "What did you say?"

"Never mind," said Martin. "It still needs some editing before it's ready for the magazine." Martin moved toward the room, reading his article over again under his breath, while Jacob continued down the stairs.

At the door to Peter's room, Jacob paused. Inside, the house leader was having a difficult time settling some distraught younger boys.

"Come boys, you must try to sleep. I'm sure you'll all have a chance to see your families tomorrow. The faster you get to sleep, the faster tomorrow will come." Several younger boys were still crying and calling out for their parents. Jacob scanned the room and spotted Peter, huddled silently in a corner of his cot at the far end. Jacob approached the bed.

"Hi, Peter. Do you mind if I sit down?" Peter barely acknowledged Jacob, who hesitated a moment before moving to lower himself onto the cot. He stared a moment at Peter, who seemed even more pale than he had earlier that day. His round green eyes were sunken deep into his colourless cheeks and he chewed absentmindedly on the sleeve of his nightshirt.

"I just came to see if you were alright, Peter," said Jacob. At the other end of the room, the house leader had started to sing a familiar Czech song. The music drifted toward

Peter and Jacob, like a lullaby.

"I want to be with my parents." It was the first time Jacob had heard Peter speak and the forceful emotion in Peter's voice startled Jacob.

"I understand," replied Jacob after a moment's pause. "But that is not possible." There was no use in covering up the truth. It was better to be honest from the beginning than try to create false hopes for the younger children. "But believe me, Peter, your parents would want you to be here. We have better rooms than any of the grown-ups have, and there's more space here than in any of their barracks."

Peter glanced around the room as Jacob spoke. Jacob knew what Peter was thinking. This room had about forty children in it and seemed crammed with beds and people. Jacob knew that as harsh as these conditions seemed, the adults had it much worse. He had seen some of their rooms: torn mattresses separated by ripped curtains, dirt floors that became muddy with the rain, primitive toilets in the rooms or just outside, no running water at all.

"Besides," continued Jacob. "You will get to see your parents most days."

"I'm hungry," said Peter, looking even sadder.

Jacob nodded again. "I know. It's something we all have to get used to. Your mom works in the kitchen, so maybe she'll be able to slip you some extra food now and then. It's lucky for you and for her that she has that job." Jacob had often begged for extra food in the food line, to no avail.

"I miss Clara," whispered Peter.

Jacob sighed. What could he say to help this young boy feel better? Nothing. Everybody had to adapt to Terezin in their own time, in their own way. He wanted to say that the faster Peter adjusted, the better for him. But he knew that would do no good.

"Listen, Peter. My room is just up the stairs. If you need anything, just come and find me. I'll help if I can."

Peter's eyes flashed for a moment, an angry look that implied he didn't believe Jacob. The anger surprised Jacob, but pleased him as well. Anger was good. Anger sometimes helped make you stronger, he thought. With nothing left to say, Jacob stood and left the room, climbing up the stairs, just as the lights suddenly went out. This didn't bother him. He was used to making his way in the dark. As he passed through the familiar hallway, he turned into his own room and felt his way over to his bunk.

Jacob undressed silently and climbed into his bed, pulling the moth-eaten blanket up to his chin. Turning over, he reached under his pillow and felt for the small loaf of bread he had carefully wrapped in a cloth and hidden there. The bread was a trophy, awarded to him for volunteering to help clean out one of the latrines. It took all his will power not to eat it. Maybe he would trade it for some warmer socks, he thought, or for some paper for the magazine. Or perhaps he'd even give it to that boy, Peter, or to his sister. He wasn't sure why he'd taken an interest in Clara and her brother. Whatever the reason, Jacob fell asleep hoping that he would see her again the next day.

Chapter Six

THE FIRST MORNING

IN HER DREAM, Clara was flying again. Only this time, as she floated high up in the sky, she didn't recognize the land below. It was grey and brown and foreign looking. Where was Clara's city and its beautiful bridges and buildings? What had happened to her home and the people she knew and loved? She was lost now, alone and very cold. Suddenly, Clara heard the far-off ringing of bells. Were they bells from the church of Saint Mikulas in Prague where Wolfgang Mozart was said to have played the organ? Or were they the school bells summoning Clara to the first lesson of the day? Hurry, she thought, fly toward the bells. Maybe that's where home is. Fly quickly, she thought as the sound of the bells swelled. Louder and louder they rang, clanging repeatedly in her ears until she awoke with a jolt, sitting up in her cot in room number six. Bullhorns blasted outside the building, awakening Clara to her first full day in Terezin.

"Up, girls," Marta called, moving up and down the centre of the room. She was already dressed. "Line up for the toilets and then dress yourselves as quickly as you can."

Marta stopped below Clara's bunk and looked up at her. "Clara and Hanna, just follow the other girls. You'll learn the routine soon enough." She moved on, stopping periodically to shake a sleeping girl. "Wake up, everyone. We must get ready for breakfast."

Clara turned to look at Hanna, whose eyes were rimmed with red — a combination of tears and a sleepless night. The girls smiled at one another. They needed all the confidence they could gather for the day ahead.

As quickly as she could, Clara joined the other girls who were lining up in the halls for the toilets. Here was her first encounter with the reality of the ghetto. There were only two bathrooms in the building to accommodate 350 girls. The lines were long and inside, the stench of the overused toilets was overwhelming. On either side of the bathroom, older girls stood on duty, carefully keeping watch in case of blockage or flooding. Clara took a deep breath, plugged her nose and quickly did what she needed to do before rushing over to the rusty water faucet, hoping to clean herself. Icy, cold water trickled from the pipes into deep black basins. Clara shivered as she scooped up a few drops and scrubbed her grimy face and hands. There was no soap and no wash cloths and it was difficult to rid her body of the sweat and dirt from the previous day. How she longed for the warm bathroom of her home where the steam from a hot bath would mist the room so completely. It was like being wrapped in a soft robe of dense fog.

Clara and Hanna rushed back to their room to dress

and line up for breakfast. Outside, Clara once again spotted Peter and Jacob walking toward the kitchen. Peter was expecting her this time. It was difficult to talk given the presence of so many guards. Peter nodded toward her, as if to show that he was managing. Just walking close to him was reassuring for Clara. They walked toward the line together, and Peter pointed at the front where mama was dishing out the morning meal.

Breakfast was a piece of bread, spread with a thin slab of butter, and a drink that looked like coffee, but was bitter and sour tasting. At least it's hot, Clara thought, shivering in the morning cold. When the guards weren't looking, mama passed an extra piece of bread onto Clara's tin plate as she had done the night before. Clara hadn't seen her father yet and that worried her, but seeing mama felt good. This morning Clara was ravenous and grateful for the extra ration. Back in their dorm, she gulped her breakfast in a flash and joined her roommates as they assembled on the lower bunks to listen to Marta.

Marta gazed over the new girls in her group. She had seen the same frightened, uncertain, sad eyes so often. And each time it was her job to help ease these new arrivals into ghetto life — to be their leader, their teacher, their nurse-maid and more often than not, their mother and their friend. Briefly she wondered about her own family and where they might be. They had all arrived in Terezin together a year and a half earlier from Prague. But Marta's parents and two younger brothers were quickly put on another transport, leaving her alone in Terezin. In the wake of the pain of losing her family so abruptly, Marta had grown to love her role as leader of the girls' dormitory.

"Quiet, everyone," she called and the room quickly came to order. "For the new girls, I'd like to explain a bit about our morning routine. We all know how hard it is at first to adjust to being away from our homes and our families," she began, looking directly at Hanna and Clara. All around, girls nodded. "We believe the best remedy for something new and strange is to create something familiar. And so we're all lucky to have some of the finest artists, musicians and scholars right here in Terezin. They're not really teachers, but they volunteer their talents for all of the children in the ghetto. Each morning after breakfast they come to our rooms to give lessons. It's different from home, and very special. Who would like to explain to Clara and Hanna what our school is like?" Marta pointed toward the girl named Eva, who stood.

"We learn to sketch and paint here, and to write poetry as well. You can't believe how wonderful it is. The teachers are strict, but fair and so smart."

"We learn about history," continued another girl. "Not like the boring kind you read about in textbooks. We get to discuss ideas with a teacher who knows everything and really listens to our opinions."

"I never thought I'd be saying this, but my favourite is math," said Erika. "I've actually learned to do calculations in my head that I never thought I'd be able to do. And sometimes we play chess instead of doing math. Our teacher says chess is the next best way to figure out mathematical equations."

"I love the music more than anything. I've learned Czech songs and even Hebrew songs," continued another girl. "We've put on plays and recitals, and there are concerts almost every week in the attic of this building or the boys' dorm."

Marta saw the skepticism on Clara's face. "I can see by the look on your face that you don't quite believe our school is for real," Marta interrupted.

"It's not that I don't think it happens, but I just don't understand how," Clara said cautiously. "I mean, back home, that is, back in my real home, Jews like us haven't been allowed to go to school for a long time. So if we couldn't go to school when we were supposed to be free, how can we be allowed to learn here in this ... this ... prison?" Clara was doubtful that a school in the ghetto could be as good as the girls described.

"That's a complicated question," said Marta. "Let me try to explain how Terezin is organized. You'll see that there are many Czech guards here to keep order and make sure the rules are being followed. They report to the Nazis who show up sometimes for inspections or raids, but don't interfere very much, as long as there are no problems. Most of the Czech guards just let us go about our daily business without a problem. We have to be very careful of the Nazi guards. They'll turn you in or punish you in some way for breaking the smallest rule." Jacob has already warned me about the one named Heindl, thought Clara, as Marta continued speaking. "But generally speaking the ghetto is run by a group of inmates called the Council of Jewish Elders. They make sure the rules are carried out according to Nazi command.

"According to the rules, teaching is not permitted. But we've discovered the guards mostly ignore us. As long as we're quiet about what we do, it's rare that anyone interferes. And we've also discovered how to be creative about our learning. Eva talked about painting and sketching. Well, the truth is we're not allowed to have paints or pencils or even paper here in the ghetto. But we've managed over time to sneak these supplies in. The paper we use is saved from occasional parcels that reach us here. We have no schoolbooks, so our history is taught from memory. Those are only some of the ways that learning continues."

Clara nodded and, though she was still suspicious, Marta had certainly aroused her curiosity. This I've got to see, she thought. As if reading her mind, Marta stood and motioned for the group to follow her.

"Enough explanations," she said. "It's time to show you what we mean. Today is an unusual day because we've been given permission to go over to the boys' dorm and join them for a painting class. Come, girls. Line up and follow me."

At her mention of the boys' house, Clara immediately perked up. Maybe I'll see Peter, she thought, and Jacob as well. Although Clara hardly knew him, there was something about Jacob that she found interesting. He was confident and smart. He also seemed to be looking out for Peter and that alone made him a valuable ally. Sure enough, as soon as they entered the boys' dormitory Clara saw the two of them, seated next to each other on some boxes. Quickly they motioned for Clara and Hanna to join them and made a space for the two girls.

Clara grabbed Peter's hand and squeezed hard. It was the first time she had gotten close to her brother since they had been assigned to separate rooms. Peter's hand was cold and his eyes were dull and sunken. Seeing him up close, Clara was afraid she might start to cry again. Because she didn't want to scare Peter, she bit her lip and smiled bravely instead.

"He's doing fine," said Jacob, and Clara smiled gratefully at him as well.

Clara looked around, noting the older children who were standing watch at the door. Marta had explained that if the guards appeared, everyone was to stop what they were doing, hide their papers, and pretend to sing or play. They would all be in danger if they were not careful.

"Quiet, children," said a middle-aged woman who stood at the front of the room. She was quite small and plump and her greying hair was cropped short. Her lively and spirited face reminded Clara of her grandmother who had died several years earlier. Her name was Friedl Dicker-Brandeis. Marta had explained that she was a famous Czech artist. She and the other leaders began to distribute wrapping paper of all sizes, shapes and colours, instructing the class to begin drawing. Clara moved to the long table in the middle of the room, picked up the pencil next to her and began to sketch. Carefully she drew the landscape of Prague with the river flowing through its centre. Above its towering steeples and castles, she pencilled in the bird from her dream, wings outstretched, eyes pointed ahead as if searching for home. Clara drew the familiar city she knew and loved. Somehow, this exercise comforted her. Soon she was completely lost in her work and barely noticed the teacher standing beside her. Clara gazed up, as the teacher's hand came to rest on her shoulder.

"I see we have a budding artist here," she said, smiling at Clara's illustration. "You're one of the new girls, right? Clara?" Then she moved on to Hanna and paused to welcome her, as well as Peter.

Clara watched the teacher move about the room, stopping in front of others to nod her approval or make suggestions. The time flew by and all too quickly it was time to stop. Clara didn't want the session to end. How strange this place was, she thought, glancing around the room. Here she was, miles from home in the midst of circumstances that had torn her family apart, in a ghetto where she and her family were imprisoned. Yet she felt more pleasure from this moment than she had known for a long time. Clara knew that if the other classes were anything like this one, she was going to like this school.

The room leaders gathered up the drawings, quickly removed a panel of wood from the wall and placed the supplies into their hiding place. Older children watched at the door, ready to warn the group if guards appeared.

Peter sat still, staring at his paper. He had painted a room that was completely black. Suddenly, without warning, Peter crumpled the sheet into a ball and flung it angrily across the room. Crossing his arms in front of his body, he slumped down into his seat, head buried in his chest.

"Peter, are you alright?" Clara asked, approaching him and trying to lift his head. He pushed his sister away roughly and slouched back down, covering his eyes with his hands.

"Leave me alone. Just leave me alone," Peter shouted and stormed out of the room. Marta, watching from the front, approached to take Clara aside.

"It takes time to adjust, Clara. And it's different for everyone here. Some children settle in quickly, while for others it's a much longer process." She could see the look of pain and confusion in Clara's eyes. It was so hard for these children, Marta thought, especially at the beginning. But she knew they would adjust. Everyone had to. There was no choice.

"If only Peter would talk. But he never says anything. He just gets angry and storms away." Clara thought back over the hundreds of times she had seen him explode and withdraw when he was troubled or upset by something. She told Marta about the time Peter's pet bird had died. He loved his bird and had spent hours every day teaching it to talk and do tricks like sit on his shoulder or fly to him when he called. One day when he woke up, the bird was dead, lying on the bottom of the cage in the kitchen. Peter hadn't said a word to anyone. He just ran into his room, slamming the door shut. Clara heard him pounding his pillow, but when she tried to go into his room, he shouted at her to get out. He stayed in his room most of the day.

"I know he's scared," Clara continued. "We all are. But Peter just shuts everyone out. I don't know what to do."

"You don't need to do anything. Talking, like you do, is good. But sometimes not talking is just what a person needs. Peter will do what's right for him. And he's lucky you're here to care about him."

"Come on," said Jacob, placing the pencils and drawings into a box at the front of the room. "It's time for lunch."

Chapter Seven

THE ATTACK

CLARA JOINED THE FOOD LINE. Her spirits brightened slightly at the thought of seeing her mother again. This time Clara would try to ask about papa. She hadn't seen her father yet and aside from mama saying that he was working in the hospital, Clara didn't know how he was doing. The line was long as usual and Clara was impatient to get to her mother at the front. But finally Clara was there and with the precious little time she had, she bent toward her mother and asked about papa.

"Look to your left, Clarichka," mama whispered back.

Glancing in that direction, Clara's heart jumped. There was papa, walking by the kitchen and searching frantically for his family. When he spotted Clara, he raised his arm and waved. His body stood tall as if to signal Clara that he was fine and that he wanted her to be strong. Tears came to Clara's eyes, but she quickly brushed them away. Mama was dishing the soup into Clara's canteen and passed an extra portion onto her daughter's plate.

"You need as much of this as possible to keep up your

strength," she whispered. Mama dug deep into the soup cauldron searching for an extra potato. Meanwhile Clara chattered on about the art lesson that morning and how much she had enjoyed it. It was wonderful to talk to mama. For a moment Clara forgot where she was. It was as if they were back in their kitchen at home, and Clara had just returned from school. That was always the best time of the day. When Clara got home, she would be bursting with news and gossip about school, friends and teachers. In the kitchen, mama would make her a snack while Clara rattled on about the day's events.

Clara and her mother were so caught up in the moment, so glad to see each other, that they didn't see the guard approaching. Clara was busy telling her story and her mother was preoccupied trying to find an extra potato in the soup. But suddenly there he was, rifle drawn, looming over them. Clara and her mother knew they were in trouble. It was Heindl, the Nazi guard to whom Jacob had pointed on the first day, the one she had been warned to avoid.

"You think this is a social hour?" he shouted, pointing at Clara. "And you." He aimed his rifle at mama. "You think the food is free and you can give away as much of it as you want? You miserable, conniving Jews! Perhaps a lesson in the consequences of breaking the rules is what you need." Without warning he pushed Clara roughly to the ground. Her tin plate went flying. The guard pulled his leg back ready to kick her, as Clara screamed out in terror. Mama grabbed his arm begging for mercy, but he shoved her aside.

His full attention was on Clara as she cringed, bracing herself for his next attack. But before the guard could strike, there was a sudden movement behind him and the sound of someone shouting.

"Don't you touch her!" From out of nowhere, Peter came flying through the crowd of children who had gathered to watch. He flung himself at the guard, throwing him off balance.

"Get away from her!" Peter shouted, planting his feet firmly in front of the guard, fists up in front of his face as if he were a boxer facing his opponent in the ring.

For a moment, the guard was stunned and paused, shaking his head. This was almost comical. Who was this small, Jewish brat challenging his authority? The guard's face was startled at first, then almost amused, and finally, dark and angry. He raised his hand and slapped Peter hard across the face. The blow sent Peter flying and he landed in a heap next to Clara. The guard moved swiftly toward Peter and hovered over him, ready to strike him with his rifle. At the same moment, another guard approached from close by.

"Leave him, Heindl. He's just a little kid — hardly worth the trouble."

Heindl paused briefly as if uncertain whether to beat Peter again or haul him away. Then, without explanation, the guard turned abruptly, pushed through the crowd and marched off.

For a moment no one moved and then there was bedlam. The other children surged forward, trying to help Peter and Clara up off the ground. Clara's whole body shook so much she could barely stand. It was a miracle she was unharmed. And Peter! Clara couldn't believe her little brother had taken this risk to protect her. There was an ugly, red welt forming on Peter's cheek where the guard had struck him. Blood trickled from his nose. Mama was beside the two of them in an instant, and suddenly so was papa, hugging all three of them.

"My brave and foolish son," he muttered as he clung to his family. "Don't you realize you could have been seriously harmed?"

Peter responded meekly. "I couldn't let him hurt Clara."

"Well," smiled papa in return, "I guess you beat me to it. If you hadn't gone after the guard, I would have. Come with me and I'll patch you up." Papa quickly kissed mama and Clara, before maneuvering Peter through the crowd toward the hospital. Within seconds, the group dispersed. Mama handed Clara her empty food tin, hugging her again before Marta took her arm to walk Clara back to the dorm. Though she didn't feel much like eating, the other girls generously offered to share their portions with her. Clara couldn't stop shaking. She wasn't cold but the aftereffects of the incident had put her body into spasms.

"Take deep breaths, Clara," said Marta, wrapping a blanket around her. "You're still in shock, that's all." She and Hanna tried to console Clara, rubbing her back and arms and gently urging her to take a bite of supper. But it was hard to calm down and she was still worried about Peter.

It was much later that evening before she had a chance to see her brother. Marta realized that Clara needed to see Peter to be reassured that he was alright. When she finally managed to sneak him into the girls' dorm, the other girls gathered around, pounding Peter on the back and congratulating him.

"You're a hero, Peter," Clara said, smiling warmly. His nose and cheek were swollen, but otherwise he was fine. The trembling in her own body had finally stopped, and while the memory of the incident with the guard was still raw, Clara was beginning to put it behind her. She was learning that in order to survive in Terezin, you had to recover quickly from the things that happened.

Marta approached Peter. "Believe it or not, Peter, you're lucky to have gotten away with a bloody nose. Attacking Heindl like that could have meant instant death or deportation. In the future, maybe you should try to be less of a hero."

Peter touched his wounds gingerly and grimaced from the sting. "I guess it was kind of stupid. But, you know," he said, "it felt good to punch that guard. And you know what? If they try to hurt you, or mama or papa, I'll go after them again! I won't let them push us around, Clara."

Marta stood watching Peter, shaking her head slightly. He was so small and had much to learn about survival in the ghetto.

Chapter Eight

NEW ARRIVALS

OVER THE NEXT couple of months, Clara tried to keep a close eye on her brother. While lining up for meals she watched carefully to see what impact the incident with the guard would have. Clara worried that Peter was going to retreat into his shell and become even angrier than before. But Peter seemed strengthened by the incident. As for Clara, she couldn't forget being struck down by the guard. It frightened her to think about what might have happened to both her and her brother. They were all very vulnerable in Terezin.

To make matters worse, five girls from her room received yellow slips of paper ordering their deportation from the ghetto. Their numbers were boldly written on the front along with the order to report to the train station at 6:00 p.m. the following evening. Silently the girls moved to their beds to pack their small cases while the others avoided looking in their direction. And quietly, every other girl in the room gave thanks that they had been spared this time. Everyone brought out something they were hiding to give to the departing girls: some tea, an apple, a slice of bread.

Clara dug under her mattress and moved toward Sonia as she packed. "I was saving this bit of tea," said Clara as she extended her hand. "I want you to have it."

At first, Sonia wouldn't take it. But Clara insisted, pushing the tea into the girl's hand. Sonia wept silently as she took the tea and then returned to her packing without a word. The crying and whimpering in the room that night was more sorrowful than ever.

A new group of people arrived in the ghetto several weeks later. The train announced its arrival in the station with a long, slow whistle. Within hours, Clara could see the mob of people assembling at the town square as she looked out the window of her dorm. She didn't have to hear the conversations below to know what was happening. Old people struggled under the weight of luggage. Suitcases were opened and cleared of mementos. Parents hugged their children, before being separated. It was all too familiar a scene.

When Clara, Hanna and the other girls returned to their room after lunch, there were ten new girls standing uncertainly in the centre of the room. Marta immediately moved forward to introduce herself and welcome the newcomers, just as she had done with every group of new arrivals. Clara scanned their faces, recognizing the fear and shock in their eyes. Grabbing Hanna by the arm, Clara walked up to one of the girls, her hand outstretched.

"Hi, I'm Clara and this is Hanna. Welcome to our home."

"I'm Monica," the girl replied, gratefully acknowledging the greeting as she shook Clara's hand.

"Don't worry, Monica," Clara continued. "We'll explain everything to you. It's all strange at first, but you'll get used to things soon enough. We all do." Is it really me speaking those welcoming words? Clara wondered. She was no longer the new girl here.

Marta quickly took over, instructing the new girls to choose bunks and get themselves settled. She knew everyone was eager to hear news from outside, but there would be plenty of time to talk later. First the newcomers had to get unpacked and settled.

That was already starting to pose some problems. The dormitory room was crowded and had been even before these new girls came. In anticipation of their arrival several extra bunks had been moved into the room. To make space for these new beds, the shelf space had been severely reduced. Now, instead of a square-metre platform separating each bunk, which had provided at least some privacy, the shelves had been cut to half their size. Not that the girls had many belongings. It was just that the girls were being crammed closer and closer together. They were literally on top of each other and tempers flared. Marta had her work cut out as she tried to keep peace in the room. Now, as Marta guided the girls to find a place to put their things, a commotion broke out at one end of the room. One of the new girls had chosen a lower bunk next to Eva, a girl who had been in Terezin for about four months. The new girl, whose name was Magda, pushed Eva's things to one side of the shelf in order to make space for her own clothing and Eva had exploded.

"No, you can't put your stuff there! It's my place. Get away!" shouted Eva, standing to face the new girl.

"I'll put my things wherever I want. You don't own this space," Magda replied boldly.

"Who do you think you are, touching my belongings and moving things like that?"

"Don't you yell at me. You're not the boss here."

Clara, along with the rest of the girls, was already on her feet, moving toward the fight at the other end of the room. But before anyone had a chance to do anything, there was Marta stepping in to mediate.

"Eva, I know this is hard, but we've all had to move our things aside for the new girls," said Marta, gently maneuvering to stand between Eva and Magda.

"I know, Marta, but she didn't even ask me. She just shoved my stuff aside, and look at the mess she made of my things. I had a special place for everything and now it's all ruined!"

Eva was on the verge of tears. It amazed Clara how one half-metre of space had come to represent all the personal privacy an individual had and how desperately they each needed to hang on to it.

"I'm sure that Magda didn't mean to spoil your things, did you dear?"

Marta turned to face Magda. How difficult it must have

been for her on her first day in Terezin to cope with all the newness of this environment and be faced with a fight, as well.

"I'm ... I'm sorry. I didn't know ... I just need a bit of space for my stuff." Magda bit her lip. She too looked as though she were about to cry.

"There, you see, Eva. No one is deliberately trying to take away your space. Let me help both of you figure out where your things can go, so that there's some room for everything. And if it doesn't all fit here, we'll find some other place for it. I promise."

With that, Marta steered the two girls toward the bunk and began sorting out their belongings, while Clara and the others returned to their own beds. Marta sighed deeply. Another disaster had been averted for the time being.

Monica, the new girl, was unpacking, careful to fit her things into her small space. Clara approached her, thinking she might be able to talk about what was happening outside of Terezin.

"Can I sit down?" Clara asked, pointing toward the bed. Monica nodded and moved her case over to make room.

"Are you also from Prague?"

Monica nodded again.

"I was just wondering, what's happening in Prague these days?"

"It's not good," said Monica and with that simple statement Clara's hopes for good news evaporated. "There are so few Jews left in the city and, with every passing day, it's become more and more dangerous to walk outside on the streets. There are gangs of boys just waiting on every corner, with nothing better to do than pick on old Jews. My uncle was beaten up by a bunch of thugs a few weeks ago. He might have been killed if somebody hadn't walked by and scared the boys away. What's worse is that he recognized a few of them as kids he had employed in his shop a few years earlier. They had respected him then, and called him 'sir.' But now, he was garbage as far as they were concerned. It's all so terrible. But at least we're lucky to have been sent here."

"Lucky! What are you talking about?" Clara asked. For the past three months, she had been imprisoned in a walled-in camp and Monica was telling her that she ought to feel lucky. This made no sense.

"Haven't you heard what's going on in the rest of the country and the rest of Europe?"

Clara began to nod her head and then shook it vigorously from side to side. She had heard bits and pieces of news, but never the whole truth. There was so little news from outside Terezin. By now, others in the room had also gathered by Monica's bed.

"My father had an illegal radio at home, and we heard reports that the German army was moving deeper and deeper into Poland and Russia," continued Monica.

"You mean they're winning the war?" Hanna asked.

"Who knows which reports are true. But if you believe the Germans, then they're winning. And that's bad news for us. Every day, more and more Jews are being rounded up and transported out of Prague. And we've heard it's no different in other cities. It's amazing that there are any Jews left."

"But where is everyone being sent?" Clara asked. Transports didn't arrive in Terezin every day.

"That's my point," replied Monica. "You asked me why I felt lucky? I'll tell you. The word is that trains going east are taking Jews to their deaths. There are death camps that were set up to kill us."

There it was again — the dreaded threat about the camps to the east. Monica seemed to know more. She was saying aloud words that, up until now, had only been whispered. Perhaps leaving Terezin and going east meant going to your death.

"I don't believe what you're saying," interrupted Hanna. "They can't possibly be setting up camps just to kill the Jews."

"Believe what you want," said Monica, shrugging her shoulders. "None of it is confirmed of course. But there are too many rumours to ignore. I think we're lucky to be here."

Clara moved in silence to her bed, her head spinning with the disturbing news. Everyone said it was not good to be sent away from Terezin. Jacob had said that the day Clara arrived. But no one really understood how bad it was. Or maybe they just didn't want to face the chilling truth.

It couldn't be true, thought Clara. Maybe the war wasn't going to end as soon as she hoped, but surely the Germans weren't committed to killing all the Jews. Clara needed to talk to someone about all of this — to try to make sense of it. It was times like this when she missed her parents more than anyone could imagine, but it wasn't like she could go into the next room and talk to them. Besides, Clara didn't want to burden them with any more worries. Maybe Jacob was the one in whom she could confide. He already knew about the transports going east. Clara wanted to hear his reaction to this report. But she needed to figure out a way to get some time alone with him, away from the watchful eyes of the guards. By the time the alarm went off the next morning, Clara knew what she was going to do.

Chapter Nine

A PLAN FOR ESCAPE

"GIRLS," called Marta the next morning. "I'd like you to line up to have your hair examined." Loud groans greeted her instructions. Hair lice was so common in the ghetto and if overlooked, it could cause terrible infections that could lead to typhus, a deadly disease. The house leaders took turns checking the girls' heads on an almost daily basis. Clara dressed quickly and stood in line with the other girls, waiting her turn for the inspection.

In front of her stood Hanna, scratching the red and swollen bumps on her arms and back. "Look at these welts," she said miserably. "I don't know what's worse, the lice or the other bugs in our beds. Look, I've counted thirty-six bites on one arm!"

Clara knew exactly what she meant. At night when the lights were turned out, Clara threw herself down on her cot, trying to close her eyes to the vermin that lived in the straw mattresses. In the morning, the bites and bumps on her body were evidence that these bugs had feasted on her while she was asleep.

The line moved slowly as Marta and a couple of other room leaders carefully combed each girl's hair with a narrow and sharp pick.

"It was so hot last night," complained Hanna. "I even tried sleeping on the floor, because I thought it would be cooler down there. Was I ever sorry!"

Summer was coming, and Clara had been warned about the effects of weather in the ghetto. With poor ventilation it was stiflingly hot in the rooms.

"What happened?" Clara asked, moving one step forward in the line.

"I think a rat ran right over my face! Ugh!"

"Was that you who screamed last night?" Clara asked. "I thought Erika was having a nightmare again."

"It scared me so much I jumped right back into my bunk." Hanna shuddered.

"Eva," Marta said up ahead, "the lice aren't too bad yet, but you'll have to wash your hair with petroleum to make sure it doesn't get worse."

All around, the girls crinkled their noses and looked away. The gasoline smelled so badly that no one wanted to be around you if you were the one infected. Still, it was better than the alternative. If washing your hair in gasoline didn't help, there was no choice but to cut your hair as short as possible.

The line resumed and several other girls were sent outside to wash in petroleum as well. Everyone felt sorry for Eva and the others, but they knew that eventually their turns would come. Some things were inescapable.

From hair inspection, Clara moved on to the bathroom lines. The routines were becoming surprisingly familiar. Even though it was sticky and hot, Clara shivered in the morning air and tried to wash the filth and grit from her skin and clothing. But the dripping cold water barely did the trick.

"I need a shower so badly," Clara said to Hanna.

"Don't we all," she replied, looking down at the grimy smudges on her arms and legs. "Maybe we'll get a shower tonight. I heard that we were getting soap rations later today."

"It won't help much. The water will be cold and we'll be filthy again in no time. It's just not possible to stay clean."

After breakfast the girls returned to their room for some lessons and then, for the next two hours, they lay quietly on their cots, waiting for time to pass. These were the most difficult times — hours spent with nothing to do except stay in the room and invent ways to keep busy. Some of the girls played checkers or chess on crude, handmade boards. There was a ping-pong table in the hallway. It was old and practically falling apart, and the paddles were a mess, but at least it gave them something to do. And it was certainly better than facing what the older teenagers were required to do. After age sixteen, children were put to work with the men and women, hauling garbage through Terezin, building latrines or guard houses with inadequate equipment, cleaning the filthy streets of the camp, or digging ditches. Clara knew that being bored in the dormitories was a better alternative.

Still others slept, the best escape of all. Clara lay on her bed. She wanted to speak to Jacob about the transports east. That was the only thought on her mind. It felt as though an endless amount of time had passed before Marta finally asked the girls to line up and move outside. There was a soccer match scheduled between two of the younger boys' teams and all the children had special permission to watch. Clara knew it was a perfect place for a conversation with Jacob.

"Look at all the people," said Hanna when they arrived at the courtyard. "The yard is packed. Come over here, Clara. We'll be able to see better if we climb up to that ledge to watch." The courtyard was a perfect size for a soccer game. Arched windows from the surrounding buildings faced the dry gravel of the courtyard's surface. Children of all ages hung from these windows to watch the activity below. Others were perched on ledges, carts and overturned wheelbarrows that were strewn about the periphery of the field.

"I'll come in a minute," Clara replied. "I'm just looking for Jacob."

Hanna shrugged her shoulders. "If you wait too long there won't be any room for you up there either." She moved off with a group of girls while Clara continued scanning the crowd.

The young players were beginning to assemble in the

courtyard for the match. Peter was one of the players. Clara watched him stretch with his teammates as he warmed up for the game. Since the time Peter had attacked the guard in the food line, he had become more bold than Clara had ever seen him. He even talked more than he had before. It was amazing that in this place of misery and confinement, Peter had somehow gained confidence. Clara waved at her brother and his face brightened as he waved back.

"If you just stand there, you'll never be able to see the game." Jacob's voice interrupted Clara's thoughts.

"Jacob, I've been looking everywhere for you." Clara was relieved to see him.

"That's funny. You don't look like you're searching for anyone."

Clara ignored his teasing. "Where can we talk?" asked Clara. "Somewhere where the guards won't notice."

"This is as good a place as any," replied Jacob easily. "The guards will watch the game and they won't even notice us."

That part was true. Permission for a sports event was rare in the ghetto. But when it was granted, everyone who could came out to watch, including the guards. Watching the game was their entertainment for the afternoon and they seemed to enjoy the excitement of these events as much as the prisoners.

Still Clara glanced around anxiously, before filling Jacob in on the details of the conversation with Monica. Clara told him about the deteriorating conditions in Prague and about the report that the German army was moving deeper into Poland and Russia. She also told him everything Monica had said about the rumours of death camps east of Terezin and how important it was not to get on one of the deportation lists. Jacob listened attentively. By the end of her report, his smile had disappeared, his face was somber and his mood grim.

"Do you think it's true?" asked Clara anxiously.

"Of course, it's true," he said bluntly. Clara's heart sank. "The Nazis have decided to get rid of us, one way or another. Either we'll all die here from starvation or disease, or they'll send us to die somewhere else. Either way, they want us gone for good." Then Jacob bent his head lower and leaned close toward Clara as he whispered. "That's why I'm getting out of here."

The crowd cheered as one of the players on the field kicked the ball hard at the opposing goal. The goalkeeper dove across the net, catching the ball, saving the goal at the last second.

"What are you talking about?" The applause and cheers almost drowned out Clara's question.

"I don't want to say too much." Clara had to lean even closer to hear Jacob. "The less you know, the better. But there's a small group of us who are working on a plan to escape from here."

Escape from Terezin! The thought was unbelievable and almost impossible. There were strong, stone walls surrounding the town and a moat beyond the walls. That's why

Terezin had been chosen as the Jews' town. Guards, attack dogs and sentries were stationed everywhere keeping watch, and the chances of escaping undetected were very slim. Besides, for those who did try to escape and were caught, the punishment was instant execution or deportation. So what was the point? How could Jacob even think of risking his life in the face of such odds?

"It's worth the risk, Clara," Jacob continued, as if reading her mind. "Don't you see? There's nothing to lose. If we make it, we'll be free of this place. And if we don't ... well ... then we don't. But I won't just give up and sit around waiting for my slip of paper to come."

Clara was dazed and distracted for the rest of the game, barely aware of the excitement on the field. Near the end, Clara saw Peter take the ball from an opposing player and begin to run the length of the soccer field. The crowd was delirious, screaming for Peter to go all the way. Down the field he ran, sidestepping each player, dodging this way and that. He was fast and tricky. At just the right moment he pulled his foot back and kicked the ball hard at the net, scoring the team's only goal and winning the game. Pandemonium broke out as the crowd stormed the field, lifting Peter high on their shoulders.

Clara wanted to jump up and down and cheer with the rest of the crowd. But the dreary reality of her conversation with Jacob had crushed her enthusiasm. As the people in the courtyard dispersed to their rooms, Clara turned to her friend.

"I don't know what to say to you, Jacob. I'm very frightened by your plans."

"You don't have to say anything. But just think about what I'm telling you. None of us is safe here. It'll take time to work out the details, so I'll be around for a while. I'm telling you this in secrecy because we're friends. Of course, I trust you not to breathe a word of this to anyone."

Clara nodded. "Be careful, Jacob. I don't want you to get hurt."

Jacob looked at her intently. "Don't worry, Clara. I won't do anything stupid."

Chapter Ten

MUSIC IN TEREZIN

CLARA'S DORM BUZZED with the excitement of the soccer game and Peter's incredible goal.

"Did you see him run, Clara?" asked Hanna, her face flushed with enthusiasm. "Did you know he could play like that?"

Clara nodded absently, but she wasn't paying attention. Though she was proud of her brother, she couldn't get her mind off her conversation with Jacob. Clara was confused and disturbed by everything Jacob had said. Not only were her worst fears confirmed about the deportations east, but now she was also worried about Jacob's plan to escape from the ghetto. She couldn't shake the feeling that he was wrong to try and break out. It couldn't possibly work and the dangers were enormous. At the same time, Clara longed to get out of the ghetto as well. She didn't know whether to convince Jacob to abandon his crazy plan, or beg him to include her. In the meantime, she wouldn't say a word about it to anyone, not even Hanna and certainly not Marta. On that, Jacob could trust her for sure.

Hanna moved past Clara to line up for supper. "Don't

forget we're going to see that opera tonight," she said.

Clara shook her head. She didn't want to think about escape plans tonight. She was going to see the opera "The Magic Flute" by Wolfgang Mozart and she didn't want anything to ruin it.

Terezin overflowed with talented poets, artists and performers. Almost every night the inmates were treated to a selection of lectures by famous professors, concerts by celebrated musicians or performances by well-known entertainers. The guards rarely interfered with the cultural or recreational activities in the ghetto, and these events were almost always approved.

By the time Clara and Hanna got to the attic where the performance was to be held, it was almost full. They had to scramble to find a seat. One end of the attic had been transformed into a makeshift stage, complete with hand-painted scenery and a ragged curtain. The performers, well-known singers from Prague, were dressed in costumes, stitched from pieces of material that had been collected from leftover clothing in the ghetto. The crude set couldn't take away from the beauty of the opera. Within minutes, Clara was lost in its charm. In the story, the hero overcomes the evil villain and frees his sweetheart by playing a magic flute. The performance gave Clara hope.

Give me a magical instrument, dreamed Clara, and I'll use it to set everyone free from this place. How could there be beautiful things in the ghetto like this opera, if the Nazis were planning to kill everyone? Watching the performance,

Clara just couldn't think about the possibility of death. She wanted to live. She wanted to go back home. Maybe escaping from Terezin was the right solution after all.

The music drew Clara further into thoughts that were comforting. For the moment, she forgot about Jacob and about hunger and bedbugs. This was the amazing thing about Terezin. One minute, you were angry and scared. The next minute, you were looking forward to something. Was it really possible to hate and enjoy a place at the same time? Clara sighed deeply as the music ended.

"I could listen to music forever," she said. "Their voices were amazing. Did music ever sound this sweet at home?"

"Probably, but we never paid this much attention to it," Hanna said thoughtfully. "Come on." She started to move toward the door. "We'd better get back before the guards start checking the streets. You know, they don't give us much time to get back to our dorms when these things are over. Clara, what are you looking at?"

Clara had stopped at the top of the staircase, right in front of a newly posted announcement on the wall of the attic. She hadn't noticed it earlier, when they rushed to get seats. Now as the room cleared out, she couldn't take her eyes off the poster. It read:

AUDITIONS FOR THE OPERA
BRUNDIBAR!
To be held Wednesday at 6:00 p.m.
In the attic of the Dresden barracks
Boys and girls, ages 8 - 18 years, are welcome to come

"What are you looking at?" Hanna asked, coming up behind her friend.

"Hanna!" cried Clara with excitement. "Did you read this? There's an opera that's going to be performed. And they're looking for kids to be in it. You and I are going to audition!"

"Are you crazy? I'm not going to sing in front of a group of people."

"I'm going to tell Jacob about it, too. He says he used to sing in a choir back home. I wonder what the parts are like, and how many leads there are. Well, I guess it really doesn't matter, as long as we all get to sing." Clara didn't even hear Hanna. She was so caught up in thinking about performing in an opera.

"Did you hear what I said? There's no way I'm going to stand up in front of an audience and sing." Hanna repeated herself, more forcefully this time.

"What are you talking about?" Clara frowned at her friend. "Of course you're going to try out. I know you can sing, Hanna, so don't try to tell me you can't. You and I have sung together in school concerts before, with lots of people watching."

"Clara, that was different. We sang for our parents, not a bunch of strangers."

"Hanna, what difference does that make? Singing is singing no matter where you do it or who's listening. Oh please, say you'll come with me."

Clara didn't even know what "Brundibar" was

about. But it didn't really matter. After tonight's amazing experience, she knew if it was anything like the other performances in Terezin, it would be wonderful. And the chance to work with talented musicians was something special. As for Clara, she loved to sing. She could sing alone, in front of one person or before an entire assembly. Being in this opera was just what she was looking for in Terezin, something exciting to take her mind off the stench, the dirt, and the lack of food, not to mention the threat of deportations. She was determined to try out for it.

Clara put her arm around Hanna's shoulder. "Hanna, you and I are going to audition for 'Brundibar,'" she said again, slowly and deliberately. "And so is Jacob, once I tell him about it. The three of us are going to be in this opera. Believe me, we're going to be great!"

Chapter Eleven

THE AUDITION

IT DIDN'T TAKE MUCH to convince Jacob to audition for the opera "Brundibar." When he heard that kids were going to be part of a performance, he told Clara to count him in. He didn't say much when she mentioned his escape plans. He said he would be a part of anything that was interesting in the ghetto. Clara knew not to push it too hard.

Together they worked on Hanna, until she had no choice but to come along. She wasn't thrilled with the idea, but she was willing to give it a try. Even Peter said he might come along, but at the last minute, he excused himself because of a nagging cough. Everyone knew it was important to take care of a cough to make sure it didn't get worse.

On the following Wednesday evening, Clara, Hanna and Jacob made their way to the attic of the Dresden barracks. At least a dozen other children were already there by the time they arrived. More appeared over the next few minutes, and before long the room was filled.

"I heard that the composer of the opera, Hans Krasa, is

here in Terezin," Clara whispered to break the tension in the air. "The opera was performed at the orphanage in Prague. Apparently it was a real hit there."

"I remember hearing about it," Jacob replied, thinking back to his days in the orphanage. "But I never had the chance to see it then. I was too busy with other activities. I guess I'm less busy these days," he added sarcastically.

"This is a mistake," moaned Hanna anxiously. "I don't want to be here."

"Hanna, think of it this way," interjected Jacob with a sly smile, "if you were back in your room right now, you'd be cleaning up your bunk and washing the floor. Now, which would you rather be doing? Scrubbing or singing?"

Hanna groaned again and buried her face in her hands. "What a lousy choice!"

Before long, the heavy steps of an adult were heard on the staircase and a tall, young man entered the room.

"Good evening, children," he said, bowing formally.

"Good evening," everyone replied in unison.

"My name is Rudolf Freudenfeld, but you can call me Rudi. Before we begin the audition, I'd like to tell you about the opera itself. This opera was first performed in the orphanage in Prague, where my father was once the director. I remember seeing it there and I know what a wonderful experience it was for the children who performed, and for their audience. I hope each and every one of you will have a chance to feel the excitement of participating in this project. Now, let me tell you about the story. It is a moving tale of good and evil. There are two children whose names are Aninka and Pepichek."

Then Rudi began to tell the story of the opera. Aninka and Pepichek go out into the big city to search for milk for their sick mother. Because they are poor, they decide to sing in the street to collect money for milk from the townspeople. But they are stopped by Brundibar, the evil organ grinder. The streets are his territory and only he can collect money by playing his musical instrument. The children are chased from the street and take refuge in an alley. That night, as they huddle together in fear, they are approached by three animals — a cat, a dog and a sparrow — who offer to help. They gather other children from the village and, strengthened by the numbers, Aninka and Pepichek sing once more in the town square. Townspeople generously donate money. Once again, Brundibar interferes, ready to steal the money from the children. But this time he is caught and taken away. The children sing a song of victory over the evil Brundibar and the play ends.

Clara sat transfixed, listening to the simple tale and its innocent but important message. This story was like their very own situation in the ghetto — a group of children banding together to defeat one wicked person, the evil Adolf Hitler. Despite the harsh conditions of Terezin, the inmates here also banded together to help each other. They might be hungry, cold, or dirty, but their spirits were strong. They clung to life, to learning and to works of art such as "Brundibar."

"Now children," Rudi continued as he moved toward the piano in the corner of the attic, "I'd like to put you into groups of six and begin to listen to your voices. There are beautiful harmonies in the pieces written for this opera. Therefore, we will need children who can sing in both alto and soprano. When we're finished the group singing, those of you who wish to try out for some of the leads can remain behind and I will listen to you individually." Rudi was well organized and easily maneuvered the children into position for the auditions. He was firm but enthusiastic.

Clara glanced over at Jacob and Hanna. She and Jacob nodded to each other immediately. They would stay for the lead auditions. Hanna rolled her eyes and her message was clear. She was still there under pressure. She would stay for the chorus audition, but that was it. Fair enough, Clara thought as they moved forward into the assigned groups.

Rudi wasted no time. He began with the first line of the opera sung in two parts, alto and soprano: *"Dear children, this is Pepichek ..."* Each group sang the line twice, while Rudi moved children back and forth between the higher and lower range. Once he was satisfied with how the group sounded, he wrote down the name of each child, scribbled something next to their name, and that group was dismissed. Clara could hear that there were strong voices in the group, children who obviously had musical training. Still, she was determined to give it her best shot. When the time came for her group audition, she sang clearly and brightly. Rudi paused in front of her and wrote something down next to her name. Clara hoped this was a good sign.

By the time all the groups had finished and left the attic, there were about twelve youngsters left to audition for the lead parts. Rudi explained the parts that they were trying out for. The two lead roles, Aninka and Pepichek, would need to be played by two children who had experience singing. Brundibar was a wonderfully wicked role that would require a strong voice and forceful personality to match. There were several other solos as well: a milkman, a baker, an ice-cream vendor and a policeman. The other main parts were the three animals who would sing as a trio. Some of the roles were very big and others were quite small. But all were equally important, Rudi explained. Clara looked around the room. From the expressions on everyone's faces, it was clear they all wanted the same thing: the biggest part with the most lines. When Clara's turn came for the individual audition, she approached the piano, rubbing her sweaty palms against her skirt and nervously cleared her throat.

"Let's see, you're Clara. Is that right?" Rudi began looking down at his sheet. She was impressed that he remembered her name. "Please repeat the following melody after me, Clara."

Clara took a breath and began to sing. At first her voice trembled slightly. But that lasted only a few seconds. This was her chance to perform and she was determined not to ruin it. She knew she could sing well, having performed in dozens of school plays and concerts. And she loved every minute of being on stage.

Clara sang the patterns after Rudi and then asked him to accompany her on a familiar Czech song. Her voice became stronger and more confident with each note. When Clara finished singing for Rudi, he nodded his approval and she returned to her seat. Jacob smiled and clapped his hands together silently. Then it was his turn to sing for Rudi. Jacob had a wonderful voice. He sang easily and strongly. Several people in the room, including Clara, applauded spontaneously when he was done. When everyone in the room had finished their individual tryouts, Rudi stood and faced the group.

"Children, I know you're all anxious to know who will get which part." He paused as everyone nodded. "I will need a few days to think about the various roles. We will all meet back here on Monday evening and I will assign parts at that time. Thank you for coming and I will see you on Monday."

Clara, Jacob and the others left the attic and moved down the stairs into the early night air. Clara was sweating and exhausted, but exhilarated at the same time. In the excitement of the audition, she had hardly realized how stifling it had been in the attic. There was no relief from the oppressive heat. Clara and Jacob wished each other luck for the hundredth time as they said goodnight. It's out of our hands now, thought Clara. They had done their best and now there was nothing more to do but wait until the results on Monday.

Hanna was waiting up when Clara returned to the dorm. "Oh, I know you'll get a good part, Clara," Hanna said encouragingly, after Clara filled her in on the individual auditions. "You have a great voice. Maybe if I'm lucky, I'll do the clean-up."

"Oh Hanna, don't be silly. You'll be in the chorus, for sure. Just think how much fun this is going to be." Clara reached for Hanna's hand. "We're going to be on stage, with lights and costumes and music and make-up. Did you ever think, when we arrived here, that we would be performing in an opera?"

"I guess anything that takes our mind off our hunger is a good thing," agreed Hanna.

Clara settled into her cot and closed her eyes. She was going to sing in an opera. She was going to be on stage. Maybe mama and papa and Peter would get to see her perform. The visions of audiences applauding danced through her head. Bravo, they would shout. Encore! On Monday I'll know which part is mine, she thought. Any part would be great. But deep down Clara was hoping for a big lead role.

Chapter Twelve

THE ANNOUNCEMENT

THE DAYS PASSED with agonizing slowness. On at least three occasions, Marta had to snap her fingers under Clara's nose to pull her out of her dreams. She was lost in a world of music, sets, make-up and costumes. Once, in the middle of sweeping the floor, she stopped suddenly, leaned on the broom and started swaying back and forth, humming under her breath. Her eyes were closed and she didn't even notice the other girls gathering around.

"Hey, Clara," said Eva, nudging her. "Are you alright?"

"Huh? What did you say?" Clara asked, coming out of her trance. At that moment, she had been taking a curtain call in front of a standing ovation.

"What's wrong with you?" asked another girl. "Are you feeling sick? Marta says you might have a fever. Do you want to go to the infirmary?"

Clara laughed in response to the concern on the faces of her roommates. "Believe me, I'm not sick. Just ignore me and I'll be fine."

Returning to her sweeping, she tried hard to stay

focussed. But thoughts of the opera were all-consuming. Clara understood why "Brundibar" had become so important to her. Somehow, in the ghetto, it represented a kind of escape. Not the kind Jacob was thinking about, but perhaps just as important. If Clara couldn't physically leave Terezin, then in her mind she might be able to get away. The only way to become free was to do something that would absorb her totally. That's what doing the opera meant to her. Clara loved singing and acting. But more than that, she needed to become involved in something important to her.

"No one can figure out why I want to do this so badly. Do you understand?" Clara asked as she and Jacob stood together in the food line later that day. It seemed like the meals were becoming more meagre and pathetic each day. Clara was amazed at how they were able to keep up their strength. Yesterday there was neither bread nor potatoes. Today, the soup was thinner than usual. It looked like the water mama used to wash dishes back at home. Clara's stomach growled so loudly she was certain the whole line could hear.

"I don't think it means as much to me as it does to you," replied Jacob thoughtfully. "But I do understand what you're saying. We're all looking for something we can get excited about here. I love it when I'm watching a soccer game. The field in the courtyard is lousy and the soccer ball is falling apart. But when I'm watching, I can pretend that I'm back home in the stadium court in Prague. It's the season finals and the entire city is out to cheer the teams on. And for a moment, I forget that I'm in Terezin."

"Exactly," replied Clara, nodding enthusiastically. Jacob always understood her.

"Jacob, you're not still thinking about that crazy escape plan, are you? I'm so afraid it won't work." Clara's fears were based on stories she had heard. In the time that Clara had been there, there had been only one attempt at breaking out of the camp. Two men had managed to climb over the fortress walls late at night. But they were caught two days later and immediately placed on a transport to the east. There was only one story of an inmate who had escaped successfully. At least, he was the one who was never heard from again.

Jacob lowered his voice. "We're still working on it, Clara. You can't imagine how much there is to plan and organize before we'll be ready. So many details to work out, so many things to collect."

"Like what?"

Jacob continued to speak cautiously. "Well, like a rope. They're not exactly lying around the ghetto. But we found one. Remember the new sentry box the guards were constructing close to the main gate? They had a long rope tied to one of the pillars to prevent it from falling. My friends and I snuck out one night last week, untied the rope and hid it in the latrines."

"But it's so dangerous." Clara was terrified of the many risks Jacob was taking.

"And necessary. So you see, Clara, we're getting there. We meet to plan at night, as often as we can without arousing suspicion. And when the time is right, and we're ready, we'll escape. I have to get out of here." The determination on Jacob's face was clear. "But in the meantime I'm doing everything I can to stay busy with things in the ghetto, like this opera. So, which part do you want?" Jacob asked, changing the subject.

"Oh, I don't really care. Anything will be okay." Clara was still distracted.

"You are such a liar!" Jacob shouted. "I saw your face in that audition. You want a lead role as badly as I do."

Clara's face went red as she stammered her reply. "No I don't ... That's not true ... I never said I wanted a big part."

"You don't have to say anything. I think I know you, Clara."

"Well, maybe a few lines would be okay," she admitted as she smiled. "Look, I'll haul garbage, if it gets me in this opera. And I know you will too."

Jacob laughed. "No, it's Hanna who thinks she's going to carry garbage. You and I are going to be on stage. And I'll bet she will too, whether she wants it or not."

Sunday finally slipped away and Clara found herself walking toward the attic of the Dresden barracks on Monday evening with Jacob and Hanna. Clara's heart pounded so loudly it felt like it was going to come right out of her chest. The three friends climbed the stairs to the attic along with the same children who had come out the previous Wednesday and waited there for Rudi to arrive. The air was charged with excitement and nervous laughter. They didn't have to wait long. Rudi entered the room carrying his notepad and music. With him was another man who moved immediately to take his place behind the piano.

"Good evening, children." Once again, Rudi formally addressed the group.

"Good evening," everyone replied politely. Let's get this over with, Clara thought.

As if reading her mind, Rudi flipped through his notes. "I won't delay the anticipation any longer. I will read out your names and the part you will have in the opera. Remember children, you are all talented and have done a wonderful job auditioning for me. If I could, I would give all of you a lead role. Just remember that."

Rudi proceeded to call out names in alphabetical order. And within minutes the results were out in the open. Hanna was in the chorus. She smiled over at Clara, clearly happy with this outcome. Jacob was asked to play the part of the policeman. It was a perfect role for him and his confident manner was just what the part needed. As for Clara, she was going to be one of the three animals, the sparrow, and she couldn't have been happier!

With hardly a moment to digest the impact of the announcements, Rudi quickly moved into rehearsal mode. First the chorus pieces would have to be learned. Solos and lead roles would come later. There were no copies of the scripts, so it was up to Rudi to teach the parts. Clara and the others would have to learn them from memory. They sang well into the night and by the time Clara left the attic, everyone looked exhausted, but happy. Even Hanna was pleased as she walked ahead humming one of the tunes under her breath. Jacob fell into step beside Clara.

"I'll never wake up when the siren blows tomorrow,"

moaned Clara. "But I'm feeling such a good kind of tired."

"Well, my night isn't over yet," said Jacob with a soberness that cut the excitement of the evening. Clara glanced sharply in his direction. She knew that he was talking about the escape.

"When a meeting is organized, we all have to be there." Jacob turned to meet Clara's gaze. "I told you there was a lot to do."

There was nothing to say to Jacob, so he and Clara walked on silently. Clara's mind was racing. On the one hand, she was still spinning from the excitement of the "Brundibar" rehearsal. On the other hand, she was terrified for Jacob and the danger in which he was placing himself. And all of this was complicated by a longing to get out of Terezin herself.

Up ahead two men were pushing a wheelbarrow, straining with its weight. Clara knew that under their filthy blanket lay the bodies of inmates who had died that day, either of illness or hunger. Following behind the cart were the families of those who had died. Heads bowed, they trudged after their departed loved ones toward the main gate. The sight of these carts being rolled through the streets of the ghetto had become so familiar that Clara no longer turned her head away when they passed. She sometimes thought maybe they were the lucky ones. No more suffering for them.

Clara turned to say goodnight to Jacob before she and Hanna climbed the steps to their dorm and disappeared inside.

Chapter Thirteen

JACOB'S MEETING

JACOB WATCHED Clara and Hanna go into their room and then he too walked into his dorm and got into his bunk. But he knew he would have little sleep tonight. Jacob lay awake for a long time, waiting for his roommates to settle in, for their breathing to become even. After the sounds around him had stopped, he waited some more, just to be sure that no one stirred. Finally, Jacob sat up and quietly moved off his bunk. It was a good thing that the room leaders for the older children slept in a separate room. Jacob had not undressed, so it was easy to grab his shoes off the shelf and tiptoe out the door and down the stairs into the darkness of the night.

Once outside, Jacob peered around cautiously, checking to see if there were guards close by, but it seemed the coast was clear. He brushed his hand through his hair, trying to calm the pains in his stomach that always erupted from nerves before one of these meetings. He was well aware of the dangers involved in what he was planning.

With a deep breath, he set off through the deserted

streets of Terezin. Though it was pitch black outside, Jacob knew his way around. Despite the rules prohibiting inmates from being outside after dark, he often crept around Terezin after curfew. It was like a game for him, dodging the floodlights, seeing how many guards he could get past soundlessly.

Farther away from the safety of the dormitories he fled. Deeper into the ghetto, past the barracks, around the kitchen and behind the infirmary. In her room, Clara and the others were probably fast asleep, safe for the time being, thought Jacob. But how long could they stay safe when every day, more and more people were being sent off in transports? Yesterday, five boys in his room had received yellow slips. Jacob was frightened at the thought of escaping the ghetto, but more frightened by the alternative. He paused to press his back against the wall, as a search beam moved close by.

Every sound made him jump; the bark of a dog, a stone being kicked. Was that someone coughing in the dark? The sound of footsteps behind him startled him. Desperately, he tried to push the fears out of his mind, but like the bugs that crawled into his bed at night, the fear crept back in.

Finally, Jacob reached a small building on the outskirts of the ghetto. It was an old storage building, now deserted except for some empty barrels. After pausing to check behind him, he crept inside and moved toward a small door at the back. Jacob rapped a code on the door; two quick knocks followed by three more, slower and spaced apart. From inside, there was the shuffle of footsteps. Then the door opened a crack and Jacob moved into the darkness of the small room. The door closed behind him and only then was a small light switched on, casting a ghostly glow across the room. Jacob looked around, straining in the shadows to see the faces of the three young men who were masterminding the escape plan.

"You're late," one man said, motioning for Jacob to sit down on the floor. He waved his hand in the air as Jacob began to explain his delay.

"Never mind. There's too much to do and too little time." Jacob knew little of the men who were part of this plot, only their first names: Erik, John and Eli. Erik was about twenty, tall, with dark hair and eyes. He was their leader, a young man who had been in Terezin for more than a year. In that time he had seen his parents and older brothers deported to eastern camps. He was determined not to share their fates. John was also about twenty. He walked with a limp from a beating he had received after having been caught stealing bread from the kitchen. Like Erik, John had been in Terezin for more than a year. Eli was a year or two younger than the others. He was John's cousin and he was friendlier than the two other men. Jacob liked Eli best. Other information about the men was unimportant. The only thing that mattered was their common goal, to break out of the ghetto and be free as soon as possible. Jacob could see the determination on each man's face. Jacob was the youngest of the group and they wondered if he was as confident about the escape as they were.

The man who had spoken bent down to lift up a loose floorboard. Reaching under the floor, he pulled out a crumpled and stained sheet of paper and spread it out, smoothing the creases as his hands moved around, pointing out several locations here and there. Jacob recognized the roughly drawn map of the ghetto.

"So, now we're clear about where," Eli said, as his finger rested on a spot on the map marking the wall surrounding the ghetto. The spot they had picked was farthest away from the guards' sentry and fairly well concealed by buildings in the vicinity. "But we still have to decide when. Any suggestions?"

"We're not ready yet," said John. "The important thing is that the weather needs to be good. Tall grass and trees out there will help give us extra protection." The others nodded, while Jacob said nothing. The nervous pain in his stomach was sharp. Finally, Erik turned to address him.

"What about you? You haven't said a word tonight. What are you thinking, Jacob? Do you still want to get out of here?"

Jacob knew he wanted to get out of the ghetto. He understood the dangers involved in trying to escape. But was he ready to risk his life to make it happen? That was the question that had plagued Jacob ever since Clara had begun to question him about the consequences of his plan. He had never met anyone like Clara before. She was strong, intelligent and brave. But she was also very practical. Until now he had made it his business never to get too close to anyone in the ghetto. Clara had changed that. She was becoming his friend, someone he could confide in. He was beginning to care about her and what she thought. Jacob shook his head and closed his eyes. He came back to the moment.

"I'm ready." The voice that spoke was his. "Tell me when we're going, and I'll be there."

"He's fine," added Eli. "You know he's in."

Erik hesitated a moment longer, his eyes moving intently from Jacob to the others in the room. Then he nodded slowly.

"Okay. When we need to meet again, we'll contact you. When we're set, we'll pass the signal to leave. Be ready for it." Without another word, the three men stood to end the meeting. The light was switched off and the door opened. One by one, they snuck out and scurried into the darkness, leaving Jacob alone.

"I can do this," he whispered to himself in the dark. "These guys know what they're doing. I trust them."

Jacob stood, pushed open the door and peered outside. A guard patrolled in the distance and Jacob waited, his back pressed against the wall of the building. Finally, the coast was clear and Jacob took off in the direction of the dormitories. He dodged in and out of doorways, around buildings and down alleys until he came to his dorm. He crept into his room and back into his bunk.

Chapter Fourteen

REHEARSALS

IT WASN'T UNTIL the following Friday evening that Clara had a chance to tell her parents and Peter the outcome of the "Brundibar" auditions. Peter wasn't really impressed, but mama and papa could barely conceal their pride.

"Do you know what the most amazing thing is?" Clara asked her family, as they stood behind the hospital. "The composer himself is actually here in Terezin, and he's been coming to the rehearsals. I've never met a composer before."

It was rare that the four of them had the chance to be together like this. Even though children were given the opportunity to visit with their parents, papa couldn't always pull himself away from his very sick patients. Papa had found this small covered porch behind the hospital and it had become the family meeting place. Papa could still be close to his patients, and the family could still visit with some privacy.

"Yes, yes," replied papa, nodding enthusiastically. "Hans Krasa is a gifted musician. I have gone to several of his concerts here in the past months. What a privilege to have the opportunity to perform one of his works."

"Isn't it ironic that in Prague, musical entertainment by Jews was banned several years ago, while here in Terezin, musical life seems to thrive." Mama looked wistful as she spoke. Clara's parents had attended frequent concerts in Prague. Music had been a big part of their lives. Clara and Peter, like many Prague children their age, had studied piano and had been taken to many theatrical performances at a young age. The laws excluding Jews from attending public concerts had been a huge blow to the family.

Mama coughed and Clara suddenly noticed how pale and thin her mother looked. Her skin was pasty and her tattered clothes hung on her skeletal frame. Clara knew that life for adults in Terezin was very difficult. While the children had their creative, learning activities, adults worked hard during the days. The children also had the best housing and more food rations. This had been the decision of the Jewish Elders who hoped to keep the children alive and healthy as long as they stayed at Terezin. Clara knew that the grown-ups made many sacrifices so that the young people could have classes, free time and extra food. But at what cost?

Clara was worried that her mother was becoming sick. But when Clara asked how her mother was feeling, mama just shrugged off the question. "I'm more interested in talking about the opera than in talking about me," she said. "Anything that brings us a little beauty or a little laughter here is to be treasured."

"We're hoping that the show will go on in about six weeks," said Clara, trying not to think about illness. "That doesn't give us much time for rehearsals, not to mention making sets and costumes. But Rudi is determined to have us perform by then."

"Well, my darling Clara," said papa, as he put his arm around his daughter, "save three seats in the front row for your family. We'll be there to cheer for you."

As the weeks progressed, the rehearsals became more intense. Three weeks into practice, the cast received wonderful news. Some musical instruments, violins, clarinets and flutes, were being sent to the ghetto. Some wondered why they were receiving these privileges. Whatever the reason, suddenly instead of just a piano as accompaniment, there would be a full-fledged orchestra. The musicians of Terezin came to back the cast, and Rudi, in addition to directing, also became the conductor.

With the addition of the small orchestra, rehearsals became even more exciting. Parts were coming together well and the harmonies and melodies were beginning to sound like real music. The star of the show was a boy named Honza Treichlinger, who played the part of Brundibar. Honza brought evil Brundibar to life, playing his role with great enthusiasm. He twitched his eyebrows at just the right moments, in a way that made the rest of the cast shriek with laughter. There was no question that he was going to steal the show with his performance.

By the fourth week, the sets were being assembled. This required a lot of creativity and resourcefulness on the part of Rudi and his helpers. In addition to having Rudi and the composer Hans Krasa on hand, the man who had built the original set of "Brundibar" when it played in Prague was also an inmate of Terezin. Frantisek Zelenka was his name and he had the responsibility of re-creating the set right there in the ghetto. Under his talented leadership the set of "Brundibar" began to take shape.

By now, rehearsals had moved to the Magdeburg barracks, where the extra space and makeshift orchestra pit provided the kind of setting that was needed to stage the production. Mr. Zelenka and his crew began to fashion a wooden fence around the perimeter of the stage. Behind the wooden fence an elaborate painting of a Czech village began to emerge. Men, women and children contributed hours of time to the creation of the painting, adding elements of a village to the scene. On the fence, they hung three posters. Each poster had a painting of the body of one of the animals — the sparrow, the dog, the cat — with a big hole where the head should be. Clara and the other "animals" were to pop their heads through the holes as they sang. With a lot of make-up on their faces, Clara knew the animals would be convincing.

Now that there was more space to move around the set, the cast seemed to have extra energy. Each day of rehearsals brought new excitement, such as the day the costumes arrived.

"Come children, look at the things we've collected here." A woman signalled Clara and the others over to look in a large box she had dragged into the rehearsal hall. It was full of jackets, colourful pants and hats of all shapes and sizes.

"Where did you find these things?" Clara asked as she lifted a printed skirt from the pile of clothing.

"Oh, from here and there," was the reply, as the woman dug deeper into the box. "You'd be surprised at what you can find around here when you ask the right questions. Ah, here it is," she said as she retrieved a worn, black suit jacket. "This one will be perfect for Brundibar. And that skirt you're holding will be for Aninka. A little adjustment here and there and things will fit perfectly."

"What are you going to do with these?" asked Clara again, pointing to some scraps of material.

"Those bits of cloth and fur will make wonderful moustaches and eyebrows. Use your imagination. We have to work hard to be creative, don't we?" She laughed and Clara joined in.

"Children!" Rudi shouted above the chaos. "We have to get this scene rehearsed or we'll never be ready for the opening. I need Brundibar, the townspeople, the animals and the policeman. Where is the policeman?" Everyone looked around for Jacob.

"I saw him going into one of the men's barracks a little while ago," said one of the boys.

"Why would he be going there?" asked Rudi.

No one answered. But Clara knew why. She knew that Jacob was sneaking off for secret meetings on a regular basis these days. He had said that the meetings happened late at night. But sometimes Jacob and his friends also met during the day. He was always careful about how he managed to get to the meeting. And usually no one noticed. Today, he had been less careful.

"Does anyone know why Jacob is late today?" Clara stood silently along with the others as Rudi spoke. Her body tensed and she lowered her head to avoid making eye contact with anyone. Jacob was beginning to take risks by making his absence from a rehearsal so obvious. If other inmates started to guess what was going on, then word might somehow spread to the guards. And that would mean disaster for Jacob and the others.

"I'm right here, Rudi." Clara looked up to see Jacob standing at the doorway, face flushed as if he had just run a marathon. "Sorry I'm late. One of the nurses asked me to deliver some medicine to some sick men in their rooms. There was no space for them in the hospital and the nurse couldn't leave her post. I had written permission to be out." It was so easy for Jacob to lie. No one seemed to suspect a thing.

"Well, alright Jacob," replied Rudi. "Just try to be on time from now on. We can't conduct rehearsals if people are missing." Jacob joined the group. As he looked over at Clara, the relief in her eyes was clear to him.

"Thanks for not saying anything, Clara," he mumbled

under his breath as he passed her on the stage.

"Quiet!" shouted Rudi. "It's bad enough you're late, Jacob. But now that you're here, please speak only if you have lines to deliver."

Quickly Clara got into position and the rehearsal continued. It wasn't long before she was absorbed with the script, her place on stage and the directions from Rudi.

Rudi had more difficulty than usual controlling the rehearsal. Between the banging of the set coming together, people yelling for costume fittings, the musicians learning their score and the actors talking over one another, there was much confusion, as well as excitement. But from experience, Rudi knew that with each rehearsal, the performance would get stronger. Opening night was looming ahead.

Chapter Fifteen

MAMA

CLARA SHOULD HAVE expected something would dampen the excitement she was feeling about "Brundibar." In Terezin, one knew the good came with the bad. The moment Clara saw her father and Peter appear during one of the rehearsals she knew something was wrong. Peter looked as if he had been crying and papa's face was grey and sombre. Rudi motioned for Clara to come off the stage. Everyone in the room became silent and Clara could hear the heels of her shoes click and echo as she walked slowly toward her father. Jacob and Hanna hovered close by, unsure of what to do, but wanting to be there to help if they were needed.

"Clara, your mother is very sick," papa blurted out. "You must come with me and I'll explain what's happening."

Clara nodded mutely and followed her father out the door, her head spinning and her knees trembling. She had known something was wrong the last time she saw her mother. Mama hadn't looked well, but Clara didn't want to face the reality that her parents, like others in Terezin, could get sick from the poor conditions in which they were living.

Papa explained it had started with a fever that mama had tried to ignore. In her usual modest way, she had pretended it was nothing more than a bad cold. But the fever didn't break. Soon it became impossible for mama to ignore the pain and pressure that was building up in her ear.

"Many people here suffer from ear infections, children," papa said as they walked briskly together toward the hospital. "It's common with a flu. If we had proper medication it would be simple to treat."

Clara nodded, remembering the times when she had come down with ear infections back in Prague. Then, papa had prescribed antibiotics to treat the inflammation and they had quickly done the trick, bringing down the fever and stopping the pain.

"But here there is so little medicine and your mother is already weak from hunger. So her body has been unable to fight the disease."

"What will you do, papa?" Clara asked. "There must be some way to help her." Clara and Peter believed in their father as a doctor as well as a problem solver. He must have a solution for this too. Surely, papa would not let anything happen to their mama.

"There is only one possibility and it must happen quickly," continued papa. "We will have to operate to drain her ear and relieve the pressure. But that too is dangerous. You must understand, children, that our facilities here are so poor. The conditions in the operating room are terrible.

Many pieces of equipment are broken, and while we try to keep the instruments clean, the risk of infection from the surgery itself is extremely high. I will do what I can to help your mama, but I can't promise that it will work."

Papa stopped walking and gathered his children into his arms. The three of them stood in the middle of the road, hugging each other. Clara had never known her father to be so unsure of himself, and his uncertainty filled her with dread. How could she be hopeful if her father wasn't? The excitement of performing "Brundibar" now seemed insignificant and far away.

"Come," said papa, releasing his grip. "I'll take you to visit your mama now. She is anxious to see both of you before her surgery."

Clara and Peter followed their father down the road toward the hospital. Their mother lay on a cot, her eyes closed and her mouth partially open. She looked even worse than Clara had expected. Despite her high fever, her face was ashen, and her hair, usually neat and attractive, was stringy and dirty and lay in a tangled mess on her grey pillow. Underneath her blanket, her body looked shrivelled and vulnerable. As Clara approached the bed, mama's eyes fluttered open.

"Clara, Peter," she said weakly. "Come here, my darling children, so I can talk to you." Peter moved forward cautiously and sat on the edge of the bed. Mama struggled to speak, so obviously weakened by the spreading infection.

"I know your papa has explained to you about the

operation. We thought it best for you to know everything that is happening. After all, what point is there to hide things from you?" Mama spoke softly and Clara had to lean forward to catch every word.

"You've been forced to grow up so quickly in this war, more quickly than we ever wanted. Still, I know you must be so frightened for me and for yourselves."

With that, Clara lost her control and collapsed on the bed, burying her head on mama's chest and sobbing deeply. It was agonizing to see mama like this and Clara could no longer be heroic. She was scared and the uncertainty of what was going to happen filled her with unspeakable dread. It was terrible enough to be separated from her parents each day. Now she faced the possibility of her mother dying.

Peter barely moved. His face looked like he had retreated back into his shell. Clara hadn't seen that closed look in months. Mama stroked Clara's head and held on to Peter's hand. She didn't try to stop Clara's tears and she didn't tell her to be brave. She just held her daughter and let her cry. Clara's body trembled and ached for all the things that had happened to her and her family in the short time they had arrived at Terezin. She cried for all the days that she had been cold and hungry, and for all the things she missed from home. She sobbed for family and friends who had become lost to her and for her carefree childhood that had disappeared. But most of all, she sobbed for her mama, who was perhaps the most important person in her life. And when Clara couldn't cry any longer she just lay there and let mama's hand rest on her head. Clara cherished her mother's touch more than ever.

Finally papa came forward. It was time for mama's surgery and for the children to leave. Clara kissed her mother's cheek and lingered for an extra moment, as mama whispered her blessings and prayers. Peter lay his face against mama's and she whispered something to him as well. Then, papa wheeled mama's bed into the surgical room. Jacob and Hanna were waiting outside and together they walked with Clara and Peter back to the dorm. Lost in their own thoughts, no one said much.

Marta was already waiting for them when the group arrived. She had been told what was happening and there was no need for explanations. Clara, Peter, Jacob and Hanna sat silently at the small table in the middle of the room. Other girls entered periodically and each one approached Clara to give her a quick hug. Everyone here understood pain and loss. They were like an extended family and each person's distress was shared by all. Clara was not the first one in the room to have a parent become ill. In fact, several girls had lost family members in the time since Clara had arrived. Together they mourned for each loss and each tragedy brought them closer together.

They waited. Papa had promised he would come to Clara's room immediately after the surgery to tell her how it had gone. The minutes ticked by with agonizing slowness until finally Clara heard the sounds of her father's steps climbing the stairs to her room. Papa entered the room looking tired, but calm, as he spoke. "She's come through the surgery well. So we've passed the first hurdle."

Clara closed her eyes and lay her head on the cool wood of the table. Marta's hand was on her shoulder, steadying and reassuring her.

"But that's only the first battle. Now we have to pray that no infection sets in and that her fever goes down. The next twenty-four to forty-eight hours are crucial. If she makes it through that period of time, she'll be fine." Papa leaned over and kissed his children.

"Come, Peter. I'll walk you and Jacob back to your dormitory. For now, there's nothing more we can do. Clara, you must try and get some sleep."

Clara hadn't prayed to God in a very long time. In fact, the last prayer she remembered was the day just before she left Prague for the ghetto. She had appealed to God for courage in the face of so many unknowns. Here in Terezin she had abandoned her prayers. It seemed to Clara that God would not want to come and visit this place. But that night, Clara prayed as hard as she had ever prayed before. She asked God to take care of mama and to make her well and strong. She begged him to keep her mother safe and to watch over her. Clara promised never to ask for another thing if God would grant just this one wish. And somehow, with her hands clasped over her face, Clara fell asleep.

Chapter Sixteen

THE WILL TO SURVIVE

"YOU DON'T HAVE TO be here today, you know," said Rudi kindly, as Clara arrived early for the "Brundibar" rehearsal the next day. "We all understand what's happening and many of us have been through these things ourselves."

Clara was grateful for Rudi's support, but explained that there was no point in staying away. Mama was in an isolation room and not permitted to have visitors. Papa and the other medical staff hoped that by separating mama from other patients, they would minimize the risk of further infection. Now, Clara needed to keep her mind off her worries. Concentrating on rehearsals was the best remedy.

Everyone was so kind to Clara. It was almost embarrassing to get so much attention. During the rehearsal, she listened intently for footsteps climbing up to the attic. Papa had promised to come immediately if there was any change in mama's condition, either way. Though it was hard to stay focussed, she tried to throw herself into the rehearsal with all the enthusiasm she could muster. But a small part of Clara's mind kept returning to a vision of mama as she had looked just before they said goodbye at the hospital. Several times, Rudi had to gently interrupt Clara's thoughts and pull her back to the practice.

Clara wasn't the only one who was having difficulty concentrating. There were so many mishaps and foul-ups during the rehearsal. By the end of two hours, Rudi was threatening to abandon the whole project if the entire cast didn't pull themselves together. It wasn't that they were deliberately trying to make trouble. It was just that they were all so excited they couldn't concentrate. The last straw came when a bench on stage collapsed under the weight of twenty eager chorus members who had jumped up on it instead of stepping carefully as they had been instructed. The group dissolved into giggles, so much so, that one boy lost his breath and began choking. Even that wasn't enough to stop the uproar. Rudi finally climbed on a chair and faced the cast.

"I have had it with all of you," he shouted above the commotion. "We have a performance in a couple of weeks and not one of you is prepared to go on stage. I will not embarrass myself with this production if it is not ready. Do I make myself clear?"

Most of the children became serious, though several still snickered and coughed behind their hands.

"Now," continued Rudi, "I'd like the three animals on stage for their lullaby and as for the rest of you, BE QUIET, or else ..."

Clara knew this was her cue and she scrambled to get in

place behind the poster of the sparrow. The musicians began warming up for the lullaby sequence. In this scene, the dog, cat and sparrow have just appeared to the two children, and have promised that they will help the children. They put the children to sleep with a beautiful lullaby. The stage darkens as the animals sing. Aninka and Pepichek lay their heads down and go to sleep as the final spotlight goes out. When Clara and the two other animals finished singing, the other cast members, watching on the sidelines, broke out in spontaneous applause.

Rudi nodded approvingly. "That's it," he said. "Do it just like that and it'll be perfect for opening night."

Clara beamed and from then on the rest of the rehearsal went smoothly. It wasn't until she was leaving the barracks that Clara remembered mama. Clara hadn't heard from her father yet and it was approaching twenty-four hours since her mother's surgery. Papa had said this was the critical time period. Surely there had to be some news by now. Clara grabbed Jacob by the arm as he walked out the door and ran with him the full distance to the infirmary just in time to see papa leaving the hospital.

"Papa," Clara shouted. "What's happening? How is mama?"

She searched her father's face for some sign of news, but by now the only expression on his face was exhaustion. He must have been up with mama the whole night and then the entire day.

"I was just coming to get you, Clara. Peter is already

here. Come inside. There's something I want you to see."

Clara held her breath and entered the hospital. What would she find inside? Would her mother be better or worse? Peter was waiting in the doorway and he looked as nervous as Clara. Papa steered them gently toward a door at the end of the hallway and opened it, pushing them inside. Clara's heart beat wildly. As the door creaked to one side she saw her mother, lying peacefully in her hospital bed, her eyes closed. The first thing Clara noticed was the expression on mama's face. It was calm and pain-free. Clara looked up at her father and he smiled.

"She's going to be alright, isn't she?" Clara asked.

"Yes, Clara. I believe she's going to be fine. We still have to watch her carefully and she will need some time to recuperate. But her fever has almost disappeared. She is even stronger than I had hoped."

"Can we go in?"

"Just for a moment. She needs her rest."

Clara and Peter entered the room and approached the bed. Mama's breathing was even and deep as she slept. There was even a bit of colour in her thin cheeks. As Clara stood there, she barely noticed the tears that were streaming down her own face. This time, they were tears of relief. She glanced at Peter. He, too, was crying, but he looked up at his sister and managed to smile. Clara leaned over mama's bed and gently kissed her forehead, careful not to wake her. And then, along with her father, she and Peter tiptoed out of the room.

Outside, Clara paused for a moment to talk to Peter while papa went to check on mama's medication.

"Peter, are you okay?" Clara asked, searching her brother's big, sunken eyes. He was still so hard to read, one moment playing soccer with his teammates and the next withdrawing back into that shell of his.

Peter coughed noisily, a harsh, raspy cough, and shrugged his shoulders. "I'm okay, I guess. But I was really scared, Clara. I thought mama was going to die."

Clara nodded. She wondered how Peter was really coping in the ghetto. As if reading her mind, he spoke again.

"Most of the time I'm alright, Clara. But there are so many days when I wish none of this was happening and I could just disappear." He chewed nervously on his sleeve and wiped his eyes with the back of his hands.

Papa emerged from mama's room and reminded Clara and Peter that they needed to get back to their rooms.

"I don't want to go yet, papa," said Peter, glancing anxiously toward the open door leading to mama's room.

"Well, perhaps one of the nurses can walk you back a bit later," papa replied.

Clara knew that her father didn't want to leave mama either, so she volunteered to walk back on her own. Before leaving, her father hugged her tightly and kissed her gently on the forehead as he said goodnight. "If you come back tomorrow, I'm sure mama will be awake. She'll want to see you and talk to you."

Clara promised to be there, and then walked out into the night air. Only then did the full impact of the previous two days hit her. Her mother was going to get well after all. Coming close to losing her mother had made her realize just how important her family was to her. Clara felt as though she had been leaning over a steep cliff, about to go over the edge, only to be pulled back at the last moment and saved. Not this time, a voice in Clara's head was saying. This time things will be fine.

Jacob was waiting for her outside. He fell into step beside Clara as they walked back to their rooms. At first, they said nothing to each other. But eventually it was Jacob who broke the silence. "Do you believe in destiny?" he asked.

"What do you mean?"

"You know, fate, fortune, luck. Do you believe in it?"

Clara thought for a moment before replying. "I think if you're positive and hopeful about life, then good things can happen to you. But we're not in control of everything. I mean, after all, we are prisoners in a ghetto." Clara turned to face her friend. "Jacob, you're not still thinking of escaping from here are you? I mean, if something were to happen to you, I don't know what I'd do."

Jacob paused. "Clara, I can't lie to you. We are going."

"Jacob, I'm so worried for you," Clara cried. "Even if you were to get out of here alive, where would you go? There are not many people out there who would be willing to help an escaped Jew." Everyone knew that the punishment for aiding an escaped inmate was severe: arrest and possible death. One thing was for certain. In a flash, the Nazis would be after anyone who dared break out of the ghetto. It would be easy for them to chase after an escapee from Terezin. After all, the Nazis had horses, rifles and dogs. And then there were the walls surrounding the town. What chance would Jacob and his friends have? The odds against them were enormous.

"I don't know what to tell you, Clara. I know what I'm doing is dangerous, but so is staying here. Think about what it would be like to be free again, Clara. Imagine walking on a city street, eating as much as you want whenever you want, taking a bath or even two in a row, and not thinking about deportations. Just imagining freedom brings me one step closer to it. And now I'm doing something about it.

"Remember I asked you whether or not you believed in fate? Well, I think you have good luck in your life, Clara," continued Jacob. "I can feel it. I mean, think about it. Your mother got really sick, and now she's getting better. Your brother practically got beaten by a guard, but nothing terrible came of it. You tried out for an opera and got a lead role. That's what I call good fortune. Sure, we're in a prison, but good things happen to you in spite of that. I don't know if it's the same for me."

"You forgot one thing," Clara said timidly, as she glanced up at Jacob.

"What's that?"

"I've got you for a friend. That makes me the luckiest

person around."

Jacob paused for a moment and then grinned at Clara. "Yup," he said. "I'd say that's correct. And that makes me lucky as well."

Late into the night, Clara thought about what Jacob had said. It was hard to feel lucky about much these days. But even her roommate Monica had said they were lucky to be in Terezin and not somewhere more horrible. Here in the ghetto, where everything was so uncertain, a little luck could go a long way. Clara hoped that Jacob was right.

Chapter Seventeen

OPENING NIGHT

SEPTEMBER 23, 1943 was opening night for "Brundibar." The rehearsals had come to an end and, sink or swim, the play was about to go on. The final dress rehearsal had gone relatively smoothly. In the excitement, most of the cast expected it to be a disaster. But surprisingly, there were no accidents. That alone made Clara slightly nervous. In the world of theatre there was a belief that a poor dress rehearsal meant a great opening night. Maybe it would have been better if things hadn't gone quite so well, she thought, arriving at the Magdeburg barracks an hour and a half before curtain time. Hanna was already there, looking a bit green, but pretending that she wasn't terrified.

"I am not afraid. I am not afraid," Hanna repeated over and over, as if this chant would lull her into a state of calm.

"Nothing can go wrong, Hanna. We're all so prepared," Clara said, showing confidence.

"Sure, nothing can go wrong — except that I can fall on my face, or forget the words or freeze as soon as I walk on stage." It was a good thing she was singing in the chorus and not by herself.

"Oh, Hanna," laughed Clara. "You're impossible!"

Clara didn't feel nervous. True, she was excited, but it wasn't a tense kind of feeling. It was more like the thrill of winning a prize or being at a great party. And the feeling of excitement was heightened by the knowledge that Clara's father, brother and mother would be seated in the front row of the theatre. Mama's recovery had been a miracle. Despite all the odds, she had conquered her illness and within days of her surgery, she was up and about, walking, eating and slowly regaining her strength. Clara hadn't dared to hope that she might be able to attend opening night. But there she was in the audience, beaming with the pride that only a mother could show for her child. With her family present, Clara was all the more determined to make sure her performance that night would be memorable.

"Everyone line up for make-up and costumes, please." Rudi moved among the cast members, calmly giving orders. There were last minute directions about scenery and final instructions to the orchestra. Clara walked over to where an elderly woman stood with a box of make-up.

"Come, Clara," the woman said. "The sparrow needs some make-up." She spread a thick foundation over Clara's face and then painted her cheeks and lips with pomegranate juice. Its red dye was a perfect substitute for lipstick.

"Are you nervous, dear?" she asked.

"Excited!" was all Clara could reply.

The house was full to overflowing. Every seat had been

taken and many people were standing in the aisles. There were adults of all ages, dressed in the clothes they considered their best, no doubt remembering the theatres they had attended back home. And there were children, faces scrubbed as well as they could, eager to be entertained and to forget they were hungry. No one was turned away on opening night. People were jammed into the attic, tightly packed together like sardines. No one seemed to mind, despite the fact that it was unbearably hot. Backstage, there were last minute adjustments to costumes and sets. Then everyone moved to take their places for the opening number.

"Good luck, Jacob," Clara whispered as the lights dimmed.

"No, you're supposed to say 'break a leg.'" Jacob managed a smile in return.

Hanna still looked nervous. "Oh no! Did he say something about breaking my leg?"

"Oh, Hanna!" Clara turned and Hanna gave her a weak smile.

Suddenly the room became quiet as Rudi moved to take his place in front of the orchestra. Clara watched carefully as he raised his hand to signal the opening bars of the music. The play was underway.

Everything went beautifully. The audience gasped in delight when the curtain opened. Mr. Zelenka had done a brilliant job designing and assembling the set with the meagre supplies he had gathered. The chorus moved out onto the stage and sang the opening bars. Clara waited patiently behind the fence. Her part didn't come until several scenes later. From her hidden position behind the fence, she could hear everything and see little bits of the action through the small slits.

When Honza appeared on stage as Brundibar, the evil twitch of his moustache had the whole audience on the edge of their seats. She could hear the children in front catch their breath.

One of the women helpers signalled Clara from the side of the stage. The cue for the animals was coming up. Clara crouched beneath the hole in the fence and took a deep breath. The spotlight moved to the fence and suddenly she was in the middle of it, singing the first bars of the opening trio. Clara's heart pounded with excitement and her head spun with the thrill of performing. The difficult harmonies she had rehearsed for so long with the other animals were near perfect, and earned the trio a warm ovation.

When Brundibar was captured and taken away in the end, everyone applauded. Jacob was wonderful as the policeman and earned the loudest cheers when he dragged Brundibar off the stage. The lullaby, sung by the chorus at the end, moved many in the audience to tears and Hanna, despite her fears, did not trip or forget anything. Clara passed her at one point backstage as they were rushing to get ready for the next scene, and Hanna actually looked as though she were enjoying herself. By the end of the play, the entire audience stood up, stomping and yelling "Bravo!"

The cast returned for three additional curtain calls and at the end, pushed Rudi out in front to receive his well-earned cheer.

After the play there was pandemonium backstage.

"That was so much fun, wasn't it?" shouted Hanna above the commotion. Her face was flushed with excitement as Clara hugged her and shouted congratulations.

Jacob pounded her on the back and gave her a quick bear hug. "You were great, Clara. Did you hear that applause?"

Rudi moved through the group, hugging each member of the cast and accepting their cheers in return. But for Clara, the best moment was when her family came backstage to see her. Mama hugged her first. "Clara, darling. You were wonderful. I've never been so proud." Though mama was still weak from her illness, her grip on her daughter was strong.

Papa was equally animated. "Who would have thought that a daughter of mine could sing so beautifully? You were a joy to watch and hear, Clara."

Peter was more shy and came forward holding a piece of paper in his hands. "It was good, Clara. Here," he said, holding the sheet up to her. "There was no way to get you flowers for opening night, so I drew some instead."

Clara looked at the slightly crumpled sheet of paper. On it, he had drawn a dozen red roses, bunched together in the middle with a big red ribbon.

"Oh, Peter, thank you so much!" Clara kept hugging

her brother, as he pushed her away.

Clara was flying and nothing could dampen her enthusiasm. She knew that performing in this opera was just what she needed, something that got her mind off the squalor of the ghetto. The message of "Brundibar" was clear to all, just like the lyrics in the final victory song:

"His days are numbered now. We face him with no fear. We are unbeatable."

Just like the characters in the play had conquered the wicked organ grinder, every inmate in Terezin needed to feel they could conquer their enemies. The cast celebrated well into the night, singing parts of the play and telling each other funny stories about how nervous they had been.

Chapter Eighteen

IN THE SHADOW OF "BRUNDIBAR"

OVER THE NEXT few months, Clara's life continued to be preoccupied with performances of "Brundibar." It was exciting and captivating — and totally exhausting! The siren still went off every morning at the crack of dawn no matter how late Clara got to bed the night before. To make it even harder, each evening after a performance, the cast had to clean up the attic. Costumes had to be carefully folded, make-up removed and scenery moved back into place. The benches had to be straightened and the floor swept, all in preparation for the next day. Rudi insisted on this routine, no matter how tired the cast was.

One night, after a particularly good performance, the cast decided it was time for another celebration. So, they stayed up later than usual, playing games, singing and even dancing. Rudi was at the piano, playing some old Czech folk songs. Jacob asked Clara to dance several times, choosing her instead of a number of other girls. It didn't go unnoticed. Clara's face burned with embarrassment and delight, as Jacob held her and they moved around the dance floor. Clara couldn't recall what time it was when she and the others finally snuck back to their dorms, well past curfew. But that night, she had the most peaceful and wonderful night's sleep, dreaming of the opera and of Jacob.

That evening was a highlight for Clara. But there were other evenings just as exciting. One day a review of "Brundibar" appeared in the weekly magazine, "Vedem." Jacob's roommate Martin had come to a performance with his pen and paper in hand. Everyone in the cast was nervous that night, as if a famous theatre critic had appeared to review their show. Everyone was determined to make their performance better than ever and to make sure the reviews would be positive. Their hard work was rewarded. That Friday, as the dormitory assembled to hear a reading of the magazine articles, Martin stood to read his review of the opera. It was splendid and full of tributes. Martin talked about Honza and what a wonderful job he did in the role of Brundibar. He referred to Rudi and his gift for directing and conducting. He even gave an honourable mention to the three animals and their beautiful harmonies. He concluded his review in the following way:

"... *At the end of this performance the hall was filled with thunderous applause and the audience was on its feet. Everyone, young and old, was touched by the sweet music and by the talented young people in the cast. Those involved should feel satisfied, for they have created a wonderful show. In the end, Brundibar is defeated because the children are not afraid. The children have won.*"

The review of "Brundibar" was posted on a board in the hallway of the boys' dormitory so everyone passing by could read it.

Soon, children on the streets of Terezin could be heard humming tunes from the opera. People came three and four times to see the show. Even the guards came, standing in the back and sometimes even showing their genuine enthusiasm for the play. The room was always close to bursting, and stifling hot, but no one seemed to mind.

The pleasure that "Brundibar" brought to Clara and the others seemed to overpower everything else in the ghetto. Even Jacob was smiling more in the weeks and months after the opening of the opera. Clara assumed he was still planning his escape, but she didn't ask any questions. Secretly, she was hoping that Jacob might be rethinking his decision to leave. He seemed so much happier and less angry these days.

The opera had been performed at least two dozen times when the first bad news hit the cast. And it wasn't entirely unexpected. After all, so many people were being deported these days to the camps east of Terezin. Each day, more and more families received their yellow slips of paper and within a couple of days, had left the camp, only to be replaced by new families. Like a revolving door, people left and people came. So it really came as no surprise when several cast members received their papers for deportation.

Leo, who played the baker, and Anna, who was the ice-cream vendor, along with several chorus members arrived one night for what would be their last performance of "Brundibar." Everyone had heard the news by then. These young, talented people were to leave the very next day for some unknown and terrifying fate. It was no wonder that on the eve of their departure they wanted to perform. At least their last memory of Terezin would be a memory of "Brundibar."

"It's so unfair," said Clara the next day as she walked outside with Peter. They were returning from one of the buildings where they had dropped off the battered shoes and boots of several of their roommates. It had taken a long time to get the vouchers for shoe repairs. "Just when you think things are starting to go well, something like this happens. Anna tried so hard not to cry, but by the end of the performance we were all sobbing." The memory of the previous night was still painful.

"What happens to your show now, Clara?" asked Peter. Peter had become a fan of the opera and had gone to see it at least five times.

"Rudi says there will be new auditions for the missing parts. Maybe you should think about trying out, Peter. By now, you probably know most of the lines and songs by heart."

Peter coughed noisily. "No, it's not for me. Besides," he said, as he coughed again, "I need to get rid of this cold so I can play soccer again."

Clara hadn't realized her brother had stopped playing sports. She was so absorbed in the opera that it seemed she had little time to think of other things. It did seem as if Peter's cough was worse than the last time Clara had seen him. She hoped he wasn't becoming really sick.

As promised, Rudi did fill the missing parts. For the next several weeks the new actors rehearsed furiously to get themselves ready for the next performance of "Brundibar." Several weeks later, when two other cast members received orders for deportation, everyone adjusted more easily.

And so the performances continued. Children left and their roles were replaced. Audiences continued to fill the hall. And Clara continued to be excited about the opera. Even the cold winter weather did not dampen Clara's enthusiasm. She was passionately involved in this labour of love, which brought hope and anticipation that more good things could happen.

Chapter Nineteen

NEWS

"Clara, wake up. You won't believe the news."

Clara groaned, rolling over in bed to find Hanna shaking her impatiently.

"I said wake up. Everyone's been up for ages. How could you possibly sleep through all this noise?"

For a moment Clara felt disoriented. Last night there had been another performance of "Brundibar." After the show the cast had stayed later than usual, cleaning up and talking. Clara couldn't recall the time when she finally got to bed, but sneaking through the streets to get back to the dorm, she knew it was well past curfew. Was it really possible she had slept through the morning siren?

"What do you want?" Clara grumbled, forcing her eyes to open to the harsh light of the overhead lamp.

"Get up and get washed. Marta wants to talk to all of us. There's the most incredible news. You have to hear this for yourself."

Despite Clara's exhaustion, she was curious, so she rolled out of bed and headed for the washrooms. Although winter was coming to an end, there was still a cold bite to the air and in the mornings, you could still see your breath. Clara had been in Terezin for almost one whole year, a fact that surprised her. A year ago she had found herself standing in this same washroom, for the first time, terrified about what was going to happen to her and her family. Today the routines of the ghetto were familiar. Clara shivered as she tried to wash the sleep from her face with the cold water dripping from the faucet. Around her, girls were huddled in groups, nudging each other and whispering with excitement. Clara caught a few words from their conversations, but it was impossible to get the full story. By the time Clara returned to her room, Marta was there, gathering the girls for a meeting.

"Quiet, girls," she said, waiting for everyone to find a seat.

"I know there are many rumours outside, so I'll try to give you as much real information as I have right now. Yes, it's true. The Red Cross will be paying a visit to Terezin in the spring."

So that was the big news, thought Clara. The stories that had been circulating for some time were actually true. The Red Cross was an international organization formed to treat those who were sick or wounded from war. Because it was not associated with any one country, it was seen as neutral and often negotiated between enemies during wartime. The ghetto was going to be visited by a group of inspectors from the Red Cross who had requested permission to visit to see how Jews were being treated in the ghetto. They were to arrive some time in June.

"We suspect that countries around the world are beginning to hear about what is really happening in the camps the Nazis have built to the east of here," continued Marta. "Organizations like the Red Cross are becoming alarmed by the reports that Jews are not only being beaten and starved, but that they are being killed in death camps. So far, the world has seen no proof of this, only strong rumours. Now, leaders from around the world are demanding to know if the stories are true. So the Red Cross is being sent to determine the truth here in Terezin. I'm speaking bluntly, because I know that you are all aware of these reports."

The girls nodded and Clara thought back to her conversations with Jacob and Monica. Since she had arrived, thousands of others had been sent away. Each inmate continued to live with the constant fear of deportation. The rumours that death lay to the east of Terezin were spreading around the ghetto with more certainty each day. Clara had spoken with her mother and father several times to try and understand the news arriving from the east. Her parents, as usual, tried to protect her and she couldn't sort out the truth. The only reality was that the word "transport" was a word that evoked fear in all who heard it.

"So you see, the arrival of the Red Cross here in Terezin could be a wonderful thing for us," continued Marta. "We are hoping they will see just how bad the conditions here are and will understand that the situation elsewhere is even worse. Once they report this to the world, the war could come to a quicker end."

"But Marta," Clara interrupted, "why are the Nazis agreeing to having the Red Cross come here? Why would they want anybody to see what's going on?" Despite Marta's enthusiasm, Clara was skeptical that the Nazis were actually going to open the doors of Terezin to a public investigation.

"But that's just it," explained Marta. "The Nazis have no choice. We believe the pressure is increasing from countries around the world to expose their activities."

The room buzzed with enthusiasm over the news, but Clara was still suspicious. She could not believe that the Nazis were going to welcome the Red Cross and allow them to see Terezin as it really was. There had to be more to this and Clara was determined to find out the truth. As always, when something important happened, she wanted to speak to Jacob, to see what he thought. Perhaps he would know more about this upcoming visit.

Clara didn't see Jacob until later that day and, by then, more reports were filtering throughout the ghetto. "The whole thing is a scam, Clara. Your doubts are probably right. I've heard the Nazis are going to make the ghetto look nice for the visitors. They are planning to plant grass and give us new clothes and even bring in more food for everyone. They won't let the Red Cross in until Terezin looks like a new place — a normal town."

"I knew it. The whole thing sounded too good to be true." Clara realized what a clever deception this was going to be. "So in the end, no one will really know what goes on here. Everyone will think we're lucky to have it so good."

"I just can't believe they can pull it off, Clara. I mean, how can they hide everything? What about the hospital and all the old, sick people that are everywhere? You can clean up parts of the ghetto but you can't pretend it's paradise."

There was too much to hide in Terezin. Surely, not even the Nazis could be capable of this kind of cover-up.

"What if there was some way we could let the Red Cross know that they're being fooled," Jacob said slowly.

"Like what?"

"I'm not sure. But what if we were able to talk to some of the people in the visiting group or even pass them a note? If we even had two minutes with them, we could tell them to look more closely and ask more questions."

"Do you think anyone would really believe a bunch of kids?"

"I don't know, but we've got to think of something to do that will warn the commission that things are not what they appear to be. Talk to Hanna. Between the three of us, we must be able to come up with a plan. This may be our only chance." Jacob's face was flushed with excitement.

"I don't know, Jacob. It seems to me that no one is going to be allowed to get too close to the Red Cross. The Nazis aren't stupid."

"No. But we've got to be smarter. We've got a lot of thinking to do."

Chapter Twenty

A NEW LOOK FOR TEREZIN

WITHIN DAYS of the announcement that the Red Cross commission was going to visit, the whole town began to change. It began with the grounds. Piles of fresh dirt were hauled in by big trucks and dumped on the centre square. As soon as the weather began to warm up, grass was laid out on the fresh soil. Flowers were planted in beds surrounding the central square. Two of the children's dormitories were assigned to help with the planting.

One day, Clara and a group of her friends found themselves down on all fours, digging in the newly laid dirt. She had such mixed feelings about this work assignment. On the one hand, the purpose of the planting was to fool the visitors and Clara was desperate not to be a part of the deception. On the other hand, the flowers were so beautiful and she had not seen anything like them in a long time. Clara knelt on the newly laid sod and rubbed the dirt through her fingers. She leaned over to smell its freshness along with the scent of the grass under her knees and the sweet bouquet of tulips, daffodils and other spring flowers.

"They're so beautiful, aren't they?" she asked Hanna, who was digging to the right of her.

"They remind me of the park beside the synagogue at home," Hanna replied.

Clara hadn't thought about home for such a long time. Since coming to Terezin, her memories of home had all but faded away. Like an ice statue, they had melted into an unrecognizable puddle. But there in the middle of this newly blooming garden, Clara's memories flooded back and were suddenly strong.

"Clara, look what they're doing over there in the centre of the park." Clara looked over to where Hanna was pointing. There in the middle of the plaza, a group of male inmates was busy hammering and nailing a wooden structure together. Cans of white paint were piled to one side, ready to be applied once the construction was complete.

"I've heard that it's going to be a music pavilion," Hanna said. "There's going to be a concert there at night for the visitors."

"I can't believe what's happening here, Hanna," Clara said, shaking her head in amazement and confusion. If she had been told a month ago that they were going to get parks and music pavilions, she would have cheered. But knowing that all this was really meant to trick the world into believing something that was a lie made Clara angry. It would be better if all this disappeared and we went back to the old ugliness, she thought again. As her mind raced, she could see another truck pulling up to the town square, unloading park benches for the lawn. There was even a playground with wooden swings that was being built on the other side of the grounds.

Peter and a group of boys moved past pushing wheelbarrows filled with dirt. "Clara," Peter called. "We're filling up the potholes in the soccer field. And guess what? We're getting brand new soccer balls. Can you believe this?" Peter was breathing heavily, and struggled under the load of the wagon as he tried to keep up with the other boys. Everywhere around her, inmates looked more alert, as if hope was being handed to them like a gift.

Later that day as she lined up for supper, there was another surprise waiting. Instead of the usual tasteless soup and bits of potato, there were green vegetables and fresh rolls, which they had not seen in a long time. Mama was there, smiling as she doled out the extra rations. This time, no one stopped her.

"It's wonderful, Clara. Look how much there is to eat. Come, let me put more on your plate."

"How long do you think this will last, mama?" Clara couldn't return her mother's enthusiasm. It was just too obvious to her that the guards were trying to fatten them up just in time to make them look healthy for the visitors.

"Who knows, Clarichka?" she replied. "But enjoy it for now. Look, there's even lettuce and it's fresh. Eat, my darling. It's good for you and that's what's important."

Mama is right, Clara supposed. She certainly wasn't going to let this wonderful food go to waste, even if its purpose was misleading. But as the days and weeks leading up to the Red Cross visit went by, Clara was increasingly disturbed by the preparations around her. The most startling news came one week later, after an evening performance of "Brundibar."

"Gather around, children. There's something important I'd like to tell you." It was late and Clara was tired as she slowly replaced sets and costumes. The last thing she needed was a lecture from the director. However, that was not what Rudi had in mind.

"We have just heard some news. You all know about the upcoming visit of the International Red Cross." Everyone nodded. Just that day, curtains had been hung in Clara's dormitory and the children's nursery had been painted, further reminders that the visit was coming closer.

"Well, for the purpose of the visit, a number of musical performances have been selected for the commission. And, just imagine, 'Brundibar' has been chosen as one of these events!"

The room broke out into an excited buzz. Clara looked around. Clearly, everyone considered this a great honour. And still, the news troubled Clara. Across the room, she met Jacob's eyes and read the same concerned look in his face.

"Rudi," began Jacob, as Rudi motioned for the cast to quiet down. "There are some of us that don't like what's going on here. I mean, all the food that we've been getting and all the cleaning up and painting and polishing that's been going on — we all know that everything that's being done is a lie. The day after the Red Cross people leave, we'll surely go back to the same miserable conditions we've always had."

"Jacob's right, Rudi," Clara continued. "We don't want the world to believe that things are good here. And agreeing to do 'Brundibar' is like agreeing to go along with the lie. We want the Red Cross to see what's really going on."

"Clara," Rudi said. "We're not fooled by what's been happening in Terezin these last few weeks. We don't believe that the Nazis have miraculously decided to treat us well, as if they're suddenly sorry for everything they've done. No. The ghetto is pretending to be something it isn't and most of us know that. But at the same time, 'Brundibar' is real. And it is wonderful. And we never pretend with our performance. We will be as professional as we have always been. We must remain proud of what we have accomplished here."

When Rudi finally dismissed the cast, it was late. Together, Clara and Jacob slowly walked back to their rooms.

"I still think we should find a way to alert the Red Cross to what's going on," said Jacob. "Have you thought of anything we could do?"

"No," replied Clara. "Maybe we should just give up on that idea, Jacob. The two of us alone can't fight this. Maybe we should just enjoy the extra food and treats while we have them." Clara was so tired of having to be grown up and brave when deep down inside she still felt afraid.

"I can't accept it, Clara. Look, if we're going to perform 'Brundibar,' then maybe we'll have a chance to meet the members of the Red Cross. And if we meet them, then maybe when the guards aren't looking, we can say something."

Clara and Jacob passed by the town square, now beautifully groomed and blooming. Jacob peered quickly around in the darkness. Seeing no one, he bent over and plucked a rose from a bush, then handed it to Clara.

"For you, little sparrow," he said, bowing deeply.

Clara smiled and held the flower to her face, inhaling deeply on its sweet fragrance. "Why, thank you, Mr. Policeman, sir." She suddenly became serious again. "Be careful, Jacob. Don't do anything that's too risky. It isn't worth it."

Jacob peered over at her in the darkness. "Don't worry, Clara. I won't do anything stupid."

Chapter Twenty-one

JACOB'S CHANCE

THE DAY OF THE RED CROSS VISIT was fast approaching and last minute preparations were in full swing. A route for the visitors through the ghetto had been blocked out and even the streets where the guests were to walk were scrubbed, stone by stone until the road sparkled in the day's sunlight. Cafés were set up along the course with outdoor tables and chairs, adorned with colourful umbrellas. Their windows were filled with loaves of fresh bread and delectable desserts, the likes of which Clara had not seen in over a year. The whole place looked like an elaborate movie set just waiting for the actors to take their places. Just like a movie, Clara knew that neither the sets nor the performers were real. Behind their phony exterior, the real Terezin was carefully hidden away.

Days before the arrival of the visitors, thousands of old, sick people had been deported east, out of Terezin. Those who were left were ordered to stay in their dormitories. The Czech guards also disappeared, having been sent away to give the impression that the inmates lived without supervision.

Anyone or anything that might arouse the suspicion of the visiting commission was concealed. Terezin suddenly looked like a friendly, picturesque town.

For the purpose of the visit, "Brundibar" had moved locations once again. The Sokol Hall had recently been renovated and it was to become home for this production. The hall was magnificent, as close to a genuine theatre as the cast had ever experienced. Suddenly there was real stage equipment — lights and curtains, and better instruments. There was a large orchestra pit and a balcony. Clara and the other performers worked through the night, expanding and repainting sets, this time using materials that had been provided in a seemingly endless supply. Nothing was too good for the Red Cross visit.

Friday, June 23, 1944 arrived, and with it the arrival of the International Red Cross. Inmates hurried to take their places in the coffee shops, on the streets or in the park. As if on cue, the shiny black cars carrying the visitors rolled down the street and stopped at the town square.

Meanwhile, Clara and the others didn't know much about what was going on outside. They were busy preparing for their performance backstage in the Sokol Hall. After a brief stop in the centre of town, "Brundibar" was next on the visitors' schedule.

"Alright children," said Rudi, giving the cue as the inspectors entered the building. "Our audience will be here any minute and we must all get into our places." The sound of heavy boots could be heard coming up the stairs to the theatre from behind the stage.

Clara hurried to her spot at the fence, underneath the picture of the sparrow. This time, she was nervous. She thought back to opening night and the excitement and energy she had felt at that time. Today was so different. Today, Clara was filled with uncertainty. She was afraid that if they performed poorly, the entire cast might be punished in some way. But performing well meant feeding into the lie of the visit.

The orchestra struck up the first notes to the overture and "Brundibar" was underway. Clara peered out at the audience from behind the fence, trying to sneak a peek at the visitors. The Nazi officers were out in full force and dressed in their command uniforms, elegantly polished and shining for the visit. Amongst them sat the three men from the Red Cross, hands neatly folded in their laps, watching the opera with interest. Based on what they saw that day, the three of them were going to write a report that would go to the leaders of the United States, Great Britain, France and other countries around the world. As Clara watched, one of the officers leaned over to whisper in the ear of a Red Cross visitor. Together they laughed at the comment and smiled broadly as they turned back to the stage. They were clearly enjoying the show.

The rest of the audience was made up of Jewish inmates who had been carefully selected to attend the day's performance. The members of the Council of Jewish Elders were there, along with other healthy-looking inmates. They were dressed in new clothing as if they were wealthy members of the community attending a typical cultural affair. Their faces were more difficult to read. They looked pleasant enough, but almost lifeless, like puppets manipulated on a string.

Clara's cue was approaching and she took a deep breath before popping into her place at the signal. She sang loudly and clearly but with a heart that ached. As always, the show was a complete success and earned a rousing standing ovation.

As the cast stood on stage taking their bows, Clara glanced over at Jacob and her heart nearly stopped. His face was bright red and angrier than she had ever seen. For a moment, she thought he was going to leap out onto centre stage and declare to the entire audience that what they were seeing was a farce. He looked like some kind of caged animal backed into a corner with no means of escape. Please don't do anything, Jacob, Clara prayed silently. You promised you wouldn't do anything stupid. Thankfully, the curtains closed and the show was over. Clara and Hanna rushed to Jacob's side.

"Jacob," said Clara, reaching out to touch his arm. He shook her off, harshly.

"This is wrong. This is so wrong. Why am I doing this, when it's so wrong?"

"What choice do we have?" replied Hanna.

"Why can't I say something?" The pain in Jacob's eyes was hard to watch. "Why can't I do something? What's wrong with me?"

"Jacob, stop it," Hanna continued. "There's nothing you can do. There's nothing any of us can do." Jacob stood there unhappily, hanging his head in resignation. As Clara looked around the stage, she realized that others looked defeated as well. They had performed to perfection and had clearly impressed the visitors. But there was no joy in their success.

Later that day, she stood outside on the visitors' route along with other groups of children, who smiled and cheered as they were instructed to do as the commission walked by. It was a perfect spring day and the sun shone warmly on Clara's face. Even the weather had cooperated with the Nazis. Clara stood next to her friends, waving a colourful banner, a false smile painted obediently on her face. As the visitors approached, she stared intently at them.

"What do you suppose they're thinking?" Clara whispered to Hanna, who stood next to her in the crowd.

"They seem impressed," Hanna replied.

Did they really believe that the inmates were living so well? wondered Clara. Did they truly believe that the Nazis treated the Jews with respect and dignity? Were they so naive as to think that the rumours of horrible conditions in the ghetto and to the east were untrue? Did they have any idea that they were part of an elaborate ploy to trick the world?

Leading the commission was Karl Rahm, the Nazi officer who ruled Terezin. Rarely had Clara had a chance to see him close up. He looked pleasant and friendly as he greeted the crowds of people with a polite wave. What a cunning and clever man he was. Clara saw only the narrow deceit in his eyes.

A group of children approached the commission as it came closer. They had memorized and practised their line perfectly. "Uncle Rahm, won't you please come and play with us today?" the children called out to the commander in unison. They had been taught well by the Nazis.

He smiled warmly in return. "No, I'm sorry children, I'm busy today with our guests. But perhaps I'll join you tomorrow."

The children dutifully moved back into the crowd while the Nazi officers continued on with their guests, smiling and waving to the onlookers, leaning over to whisper into the ears of the visiting inspectors, pointing out this sight or that display. How pleased they must be with themselves, Clara thought as the commission moved closer and closer to where she was standing. What a brilliant fantasy they had created.

The commission was nearly in front of her when the group suddenly stopped and pointed in the direction of where Hanna, Jacob and Clara stood. They huddled for a moment, talking with the Nazi officers and then walked straight over and stood in front of Jacob. Every nerve in Clara's body ignited with fear and anticipation. What was happening? Why had they approached Jacob? Had someone overheard his conversations about trying to alert the inspectors?

One of the men, a representative from Denmark, stepped forward and spoke directly to Jacob. "What is your name, young man?" he asked.

Jacob was quiet for a moment before stammering out his name. He looked as shocked as Clara, particularly when the inspector asked his next question.

"Tell me, Jacob," the inspector said, "what is it like to live here these days?"

There was dead silence as the question hung in the air.

"Well," began Jacob, nervously clearing his throat. "Things are ... I mean they're ... you see we're ... they're ..." Jacob's eyes were open as wide and round as saucers, darting everywhere around him as if to press the visitors to look more closely at what they were seeing. Don't you under-stand that it's impossible for me to speak? I'm trapped. I beg you to look around and see the truth. Look behind that building and you'll see sickness. Look around that corner and you'll see starvation. Nothing here is as it appears. Clara could read the message in Jacob's eyes as clearly as if he were speaking the words aloud. But she was the only one who heard these unspoken words.

"Things are ... okay ... I guess," Jacob finally blurted. "They're fine. Fine!"

The visitors smiled their approval and moved on with their hosts. They didn't ask another question. They never looked beyond what they were being instructed to see. As for Jacob, he looked even more defeated than he had looked on the stage of the Sokol Theatre after the performance of "Brundibar" earlier that day. Another chance gone, his whole body seemed to say.

But had this really been the golden opportunity they had hoped for? Nazi officers with the power to make life and death decisions surrounded Clara and her friends. There was no freedom in the ghetto, not even in that moment. They were caged animals, briefly released from their cages but still held captive on a tight leash. No one had stopped the Nazis from imprisoning Jews in Terezin, Clara realized, and no one was going to stop them now.

Later that day Clara heard the news that the commission had been very impressed with everything they had seen. While they admitted that all circumstances in this part of Europe were difficult given the war that was raging, they concluded that conditions at Terezin were fair and Jews were living in a lovely and clean little town.

Clara sat with Jacob well into the night, comforting him and assuring him that there was nothing he could have done.

"I had my chances and I blew them," said Jacob, his face pale and tired.

"What did you think you were going to do, Jacob?" Clara asked. "Start shouting the truth in the middle of the street? The Nazis would have been on top of you in a second."

"Maybe it would have been worth it," said Jacob. "The inspectors couldn't have ignored something like that."

"They would have said you were crazy. Face it, Jacob," said Clara. "There was never a real chance to do anything. This is not your fault. We were fooling ourselves to think something was possible."

Jacob took a deep breath and turned to Clara. "My friends and I are leaving, Clara. Two days from now. I've got to get out of here. Now, more than ever."

Clara gazed solemnly back at Jacob. She was more afraid for him than she could say. He looked like someone who didn't care about life anymore. It was a dangerous way to be. In the ghetto, you had to fight to live. You couldn't give up. But the spirit seemed to have gone out of Jacob. There was nothing helpful Clara could say and the two friends sat silently.

The very next day, the pavilion in the centre square of the town was disassembled and Czech guards reappeared on the streets of Terezin. Thousands of people received orders to report for deportation, as if their presence was no longer needed for any deceptive purpose. Terezin quickly returned to the state in which it had been before the Red Cross visit.

Chapter Twenty-two

JACOB

THE NIGHT AIR was cool and refreshing, a welcome relief from the intense heat inside the building where Jacob had just finished his last performance of "Brundibar." He bent to wind the thin blanket pieces around his worn boots. At night, every sound echoed in the ghetto. Then, glancing around cautiously, Jacob began to walk away from the barracks. He moved briskly, but inside his heart was pounding wildly and the voices in his head were deafening.

The last two days had felt like a nightmare and saying goodbye to Clara had been more painful than he had ever expected. Since the Red Cross visit, they had avoided each other. But tonight, after the show, Jacob approached Clara and the sadness in her eyes pierced through his. Never had Jacob felt so alone or unsure of himself.

"This is it, Clara. It's time." Even as he spoke, the uncertainty in Jacob's voice was overwhelming. Jacob's eyes were dark and tired and weary lines circled his mouth, making him look like he had somehow aged into an old man.

"Remember that time I asked you if you believed in fate

or luck?" he asked. Clara nodded. "Well, I guess my destiny is different from yours."

"Jacob, you're strong," Clara insisted. "And you're smart and brave. If anyone is going to be okay, I know it's you. I believe it with all my heart. And you also have to believe it." It was true that Jacob had always been determined and energetic. It was that strength that had helped him in the ghetto. Now he was going to need it more than ever.

"We had such a great time in 'Brundibar,' didn't we, Clara?" asked Jacob somewhat wistfully, as they stood facing each other in the attic of the Magdeburg barracks. "Sometimes I think if it wasn't for that, I don't know what I would have done here." Jacob was right. The opera had lifted their spirits in a way they never dreamed possible. It made them feel normal and alive and valued.

"You're a great friend, Clara," Jacob continued, looking into Clara's eyes. "No, even more than a friend."

"Jacob, I don't know how I could have managed here without you." Clara threw her arms around him. "No one can beat you, Jacob. You mustn't let them. You have to be stronger than they are. We will see each other again." She struggled to make her voice even. "Good luck, Jacob. Please be careful."

Jacob held Clara, feeling her hot tears on his neck. "Goodbye, Clara," he whispered and then pulled himself away.

Clara watched as Jacob moved toward the door. At the last moment, he turned and stared at her, an agonizing gaze that betrayed his own fear. Clara closed her eyes, so she would not have to watch Jacob walk through the door.

Now the uncertainty of what he was doing pounded in Jacob's head as he walked farther and farther away from the barracks. How could he have let things go so far? He had never faced anything this life-threatening before and the fear of what might happen was closing in on him. His lungs felt constricted and he had trouble catching his breath.

Jacob paused and pressed up against a wall as the beam of a searchlight moved close by. His legs felt heavier than the bags of dirt he often hauled through the ghetto when the guards were building. Even though he was moving quickly, it felt like he was in slow motion. Up ahead, he finally spotted his three friends. Fighting every urge to run in the opposite direction, he sprinted forward to join them at the wall.

The group had picked the perfect spot for their escape. At this part of the wall, there were no lights, and the sentries only passed by every half hour or so. There was even a piece of pipe sticking out of the top of the wall where they could hook the rope they carried. It had taken months to scout the ghetto, looking for an ideal exit point. But the time had been well spent. They had taken care of all the details.

"Jacob, we've been waiting for you. What took you so long?" Jacob could hear the irritation in Erik's voice as he sank into the shadows close to them.

"It was the opera," Jacob whispered in reply. "I couldn't get away any sooner without being noticed."

The opera! Had he really just finished performing a few short hours ago? For a moment, he thought of Clara. Jacob had always been alone, taking care of himself and not relying on anyone else. Now, it had been painful to choose between his friend and freedom. Jacob closed his eyes trying desperately to push those thoughts out of his head. He needed to stay focussed on the task at hand.

"We need every second to make this plan work," Erik continued, as he worked furiously to tie a loop in the end of the rope. Glancing around, he moved a short distance from the wall and swung the rope up toward the pipe protruding from the top. He missed on the first try and then again on the second. Jacob held his breath as Erik swung a third time. The rope finally connected with the pipe. He gave a strong pull to make sure it was secure.

"I'll go first. Jacob, you'll come after me and then the two of you will follow," Erik said, indicating to the others.

Up he went without hesitation, while the others peered through the darkness to make sure no one was there. Jacob counted the minutes before the guards would return to check this part of the wall. It would be close. Ninety seconds to scale the wall on this side, grab the pipe at the top and swing your legs over. Ninety more to pull the rope to the other side and move down, then jump out to avoid the barbed wire and the moat. One, two, three minutes. Several times they heard the sound of pebbles falling. Would there be guards waiting on the other side ready to shoot?

Finally, the rope was thrown back to the inner side, a

sign that the first of his companions had made it. Then, it was Jacob's turn. He took a deep breath and moved forward to grab hold of the rope, placing one foot on the wall. This was it. If all went well, he would soon be free and would never see the inside of Terezin again. If the plan failed, he would be arrested or killed. Either way, he would never see Clara again, or Hanna or Peter or any of the other friends he had made at Terezin. He would never again perform the opera "Brundibar," or see Rudi or sing again. Suddenly, he couldn't move.

"Go," Eli whispered. "Move, you have to move!"

Jacob shook his head and set his shoulders squarely. But still he didn't budge. It was as if his feet were glued in place and his hands were stuck to the rope. Jacob was frozen.

"Go, Jacob. If you don't do it now, it will be too late. Just do it." Eli whispered even louder. Both remaining men moved toward Jacob and shoved him. Desperately they tried to lift him up the wall, to give him a start in the right direction.

Even though Jacob's body had stopped, his mind was racing. The fear of what was out there overwhelmed him. Every muscle in his body seemed to be holding him back. He was scared, more scared than he thought possible, terrified the plan would fail and terrified of the consequences. Sweat stung his eyes and breathing was painful. It was much like the moment in front of the Red Cross visitors when he had been unable to speak.

Again he shook his head, more violently this time. Stop

it, the voice inside Jacob's head shouted. You know what you have to do. Jacob knew he might die trying to escape, but at least he would be outside the walls and not enslaved inside.

"What's the matter with you? Jacob, there's no time left!" The voices of the men rose in desperation as they swore and threatened Jacob. "If you don't go now, then we're going to leave you behind."

Wiping the sweat from his forehead, Jacob took another deep breath and swung himself up the wall and over the top, pulling the rope after him. Hand over hand, he moved down the rope. Metre by metre, until there was no more rope left. And then with a final push of his wrapped boots against the wall, he dropped into the bushes and pressed himself against the ground. One, two, three more minutes and the third man lay panting in the grass next to him. Then, three more agonizing minutes, and they were all out.

Now, without a moment's hesitation, Jacob and the others crawled through the tall grass, keeping themselves as low to the ground as possible. Jacob knew that only when they reached the railway tracks, would they be able to stand and run. And run they would, knowing they would have to get as far away from Terezin as possible in the dark.

Jacob turned his head for one last look at the ghetto wall. His determination began to return. He could smell freedom, but its taste was bittersweet. Goodbye, Clara, he whispered into the night mist. And then he turned to follow his companions into the darkness.

Chapter Twenty-three

THE MARCH TO THE FIELD

"GIRLS, GET UP. The siren's blowing early today and we must assemble outside." Marta moved urgently up and down the centre of the room. She paused every now and then to shake a sleeping girl.

"What now?" Clara groaned, rubbing her tired eyes. "Why do we have to get up now?"

Clara was exhausted. Surely only minutes had passed since she had fallen asleep. And now there was the unrelenting sirens and Marta's persistent orders to get up.

"Why? What's wrong, Marta?"

"Is someone in trouble?"

"Is someone sick?"

"What's happening?"

One by one, the girls struggled to open their eyes. Fear crept into their questions. As much as Clara hated the mundane, daily routines, a change in the routine often spelled trouble and trouble was something they all wanted to avoid. Why were the guards making them get up earlier than usual? And why did they have to go outside immediately?

"There's some talk that several inmates have escaped from the ghetto. The guards are furious and they're insisting on doing an accurate count of all inhabitants of Terezin. Now please, girls, stop asking questions. Get up quickly and line up at the door when you're ready, so we can go outside as a group."

Jacob! Clara must have gasped out loud because several girls glanced curiously in her direction. The vision of Jacob walking out the door of the Magdeburg barracks was still fresh in her mind.

Outside in the rain, thousands of people were already assembled. "Get into line!" the guards shouted, their rifles at the ready. "Stop talking and move ahead!" Half-sleeping children and old, frail men and women were pushed ahead roughly. Clara strained her neck in all directions, looking for someone who could tell her something, anything. But there was no one she knew anywhere in sight, not her parents, not Peter and, of course, not Jacob.

"Try to stay together," called Marta, as Clara grabbed Hanna's hand. The guards were moving them forward, shouting at them to march quickly. To make matters worse, it was cold and the fine drizzle was turning the road into a muddy and treacherous mess. All around, adults and children slipped and fell, only to be dragged to their feet and pulled forward by those around them. Even though it was cold, she could feel the sweat roll down her back as she raced to keep up with her group.

Clara could not stop thinking about Jacob. Where was

he now? Was he safe? Had he been caught? The questions raced through her mind.

"Clara!" a voice called from behind.

"Peter!" She was so relieved to see her brother. "Do you know anything about what's going on?"

Peter shook his head, coughing harshly. "Not much. My house leader says we're being marched out to a field behind Bohusovice, where the train station is. That's where the soldiers are going to count us. They seem to think there are some people missing."

Peter's chest cold had still not cleared up and he looked weaker than ever. Clara regarded her brother anxiously. Papa had given Peter every medication he had, to no avail, and this dampness was the worst possible thing for Peter.

"But Peter, there are thousands and thousands of inmates here. How will the soldiers ever manage to count us all?"

Peter shrugged his shoulders, chewing nervously on his sleeve. "I guess that's why they need a big field to hold us in."

"Do they know anything about the people who escaped?" asked Hanna, who had fallen in beside them. Peter shook his head.

On they marched, past the wall surrounding the town, over the bridge and along the winding road toward the railway line, retracing the steps that had first brought Clara into the ghetto. And still there was no sign of Jacob. Clara couldn't say anything to Hanna or to Peter. She couldn't tell anyone what she knew of Jacob's plot. That would place Jacob in even more danger, not to mention the trouble it would cause for her. She had to find out what was happening without saying anything about what she knew.

Clara and the others finally arrived at the field beyond the station where more soldiers were waiting, shouting at the hordes of people to move ahead quickly.

"Line up in rows of ten for the count," a guard shouted, swinging a stick at his side. "Quiet! Stop your talking! Line up quickly!" Hanna screamed as the guard pushed her roughly into a line. "I said line up!"

The inmates tried their best to gather into lines, as the soldiers moved among them, counting. But with so many people, it was impossible for the count to be accurate. Every time the soldiers turned their backs, some individual inmates would rush off in search of family members. Clara couldn't see her parents, but at least she knew her brother and her roommates were close by.

Up and down the rows of people the soldiers marched, swinging their sticks and pointing their rifles. Again and again they counted, shouting for quiet. More than fifty times they repeated this exercise, but still they were not satisfied. They would finish inspecting the lines and move away, only to return within a few minutes and order everyone to line up again. The hours went by and still there was no sign of returning to the ghetto. Hunger gripped and gnawed at her stomach and she longed for food and water. All around her, weary inmates slumped to the ground, unable to stand any longer. And finally Clara also sank down on the grass and stared out into the mist, past the trees in the distance.

It was getting dark and cold again and everyone was soaking wet. Clara suddenly realized that they had been out in the field for the entire day. She tried to see beyond the outskirts of the field as the noises around her faded. Was Jacob out there somewhere? Was he free from Terezin? What would it be like to escape this place and stroll freely out in the woods? Clara wondered. Somewhere out there, past the forest, there were comfortable beds, clean clothes and hot baths. Would she ever feel those comforts again? Would she ever have that freedom?

"I want to go back to our rooms," whimpered Hanna.

Clara snickered. "Listen to what you're saying. Are you actually wishing you were back in the ghetto?" It didn't make sense that they were living their lives this way. But in their dorm, they would be warm again. Warmth was better than cold; cold was better than hunger; hunger was better than being away from parents. And being in Terezin was better than being out here. The world was upside down and nothing made sense anymore. It was okay to imprison her family and friends, but you could be punished for trying to help. Wrong was right and right was wrong. It was impossible to even think about the future because no one really knew if they had one. Every prisoner in Terezin lived only to get through one day at a time. And so Clara sat in the field, trying to get through yet another trial, while, all around her, the count continued.

Clara never knew who finally gave the order to return to the ghetto. But like a great wave that moves from the sea onto the sand, a flood of people suddenly began to surge toward the town, pushing and shoving in the cold night air. Hanna grabbed Clara's arm and she in turn pulled Peter to his feet before they could all be crushed by the masses. Within seconds Clara was being swept along, her feet barely touching the ground as the crowd pressed forward. Children cried as they lost hold of their house leaders. Old women and men fell, unable to keep up with the rush of inmates. Orders were given for the inmates to pick up the elderly and drag them back. Clara was terrified. Somehow she and her friends managed to stay together and returned to their building. The time was close to midnight.

Before they entered, Clara caught a glimpse of her brother approaching the boys' dormitory. Clara ran over to him. As Clara hugged him, she could feel him shivering. He felt hot and feverish and he promised he would try to see papa in the morning for more medicine. For now Clara thought that sleep was the thing he and everyone needed most. Peter walked slowly up the stairs into his dormitory, looking sick and miserable.

Now Clara was too tired to think about anything. She and Hanna entered their room and fell into their beds. One by one, the other girls returned, their pale faces numbed by the events of the day. No one bothered undressing and no one spoke.

The following day, the siren went off as usual and Clara returned to her regular routine. No one really talked much about the march to the field. There was no point in dwelling on it. To survive in Terezin, you had to get through each day at a time. That day, eight girls in Clara's room received deportation orders. The familiar yellow slips of paper were waiting for them when they returned from breakfast.

The soldiers never really managed to figure out how many prisoners there were in Terezin. Hundreds of people had died in the march to the field. For the next two weeks, everyone had to walk in lines on the street and no one was allowed outside after 6:00 p.m. After two weeks had passed, the curfew was lifted. A performance of "Brundibar" was scheduled and Clara and the rest of the cast all jumped back into their roles.

Clara never learned what had become of Jacob and his friends. An escape had not been formally announced. Meanwhile, another young boy replaced him as the policeman in the opera and the show continued. And every day Clara prayed that Jacob was safe and free.

Chapter Twenty-four

PETER

TWO WEEKS PASSED and Peter's chest infection was not improving. No matter what papa did, Peter seemed to be getting more and more sick.

"Papa is going to move Peter to the hospital today," whispered mama one morning in the food line, as she poured weak coffee into Clara's cup. "It's not only for Peter's sake, but we're afraid the other children in his room will also become ill."

Clara knew that infections could spread quickly in the ghetto. One day, one person would be sick and before you knew it, a whole room full of people would follow.

"He's going to be alright, isn't he, mama?" asked Clara.

Mama hesitated before speaking. "Papa is doing everything he can. Look how well I became under his care. But Peter needs our prayers, Clarichka."

Mama spoke with such uncertainty that it frightened Clara. As soon as she could, she snuck out to the hospital so she could see Peter for herself. Being in a hospital wasn't new for Clara. She had visited her father's clinic in Prague many times and seen people who were ill or in pain. In Terezin, she was familiar with the hospital from her mother's illness. But this time, as Clara entered the clinic, she knew it was different.

As soon as she walked through the door of the hospital, she was overwhelmed by the smell of sickness and death. The room was filled with bunks, occupied by old men and women, many groaning weakly. They looked as though they were wasting away, their cheeks hollow and their eyes sunken and empty. Clara froze in complete terror, staring at the scene in front of her.

"Clara," a nurse said, recognizing her. She gently took Clara by the arm and maneuvered her toward a door at the back. "Peter's in an isolation room. Your father is with him now, and you won't be able to go in. There's too much risk of the infection spreading. But you can see him through this window."

"What's ... what's the matter with everyone here?" Clara asked, gesturing back to the main room. "I mean, they all look like they're dying."

"The people in this room are very sick, and there's very little we can do for them. We just try to keep them as comfortable as possible for their last days." The nurse rushed back to one of the patients who had suddenly cried out. Clara approached the window to look in on her brother. She was still shaken by what she had seen, and the sight of Peter lying in his hospital cot did little to help.

Clara gasped as she pressed her hands and face against

the small glass window separating her from the isolation room. Peter looked awful! She had no idea how sick he had become. The illness had worn away his already thin body, and he looked shrunken and wasted. Only his cheeks glowed with the fever that was consuming him. Clara watched Peter's chest rise and fall in quick, shallow movements as if each breath was painful and exhausting. Papa hovered over his son, feeling his pulse and watching his laboured breathing. Suddenly Peter's tiny body erupted in a coughing spasm. His head shook violently and his arms thrashed as he struggled for air. Papa and the nurses moved forward to hold his head up and make his breathing easier. Agonizing minutes passed until the coughing spasm finally passed and Peter's weakened body collapsed back on the bed. Clara pushed her face even closer to the window, straining to see the movement in Peter's chest. Each breath seemed smaller and more painful than the one before.

Clara turned and ran from the infirmary. She had to get away, far away. This was a nightmare and she had to escape. There was no one to help her anymore. Jacob was gone and even though Clara hoped daily that he was safe, at this moment, she selfishly wanted him back. Mama and papa were already sick with worry, and besides, Peter needed them more than ever. Clara ran through the streets of Terezin, dodging this way and that, blinded by the tears that streamed from her eyes. She didn't even care about the possibility of running into a guard. She wanted freedom. She wanted peace of mind. She wanted to feel safe again.

But she could find none of these and eventually she found herself standing once more in front of the hospital.

Mama was inside Peter's room, sitting next to him on the bed and holding his hand. Though there was the risk of infection, mama needed to be close to her son, her youngest. Through the glass, Clara strained to hear what she was saying to Peter.

"Once, in a land far away, there lived a family of fireflies. By day, they slept, deep in their forest treehouse. But at night, they came out and flew throughout the woods with the other fireflies that lived with them. And they lit up the night sky with their brilliant glow ..." It was Peter's favourite story. Clara barely noticed papa, who had come to stand next to her until she felt his arm on her shoulder.

"There are some things I am not able to fix, Clara." Clara glanced at her father. He looked like a broken man. The strength that Clara had always relied on seemed to have disappeared. Papa could no longer protect his family.

Inside the room, Peter's chest rose and fell with difficulty and the space between each breath became longer and longer. Finally, Clara watched as mama lifted Peter's feeble body into her arms and then Clara knew that he was gone.

She didn't cry anymore. It seemed the tears had dried up inside her body. She just watched as mama continued to rock Peter in her arms and whisper his favourite story into his ears. Finally, the nurses came forward with helpers, whose job it was to remove the bodies from the hospital. Mama kissed Peter's face one last time and then finally released her son.

The next day Clara, mama and papa joined the line of families following after the carts that rolled through the streets of Terezin. The carts held the bodies of those who had died. Peter was one of dozens that day. Hanna walked with Clara, holding her hand. At the wall of the ghetto, the line came to a halt as the wagons were pushed outside and toward the cemetery. This was as far as the mourners could go. As Clara watched the wheelbarrows move through the gates of the ghetto, she could not help but think that Peter, like Jacob, was on the outside now. And hopefully like Jacob, Peter's spirit was now free.

Chapter Twenty-five

HANNA

CLARA REMAINED in a daze for weeks following Peter's death. It was as if what little hope she had left had been completely broken. Not even the rumours of an end to the war could lift Clara's disheartened mood.

"Clara, the news reports are fantastic," Marta told her one day as they walked to get their food. Clara looked thinner than she had in the past. Her appetite had become as depressed as her spirit. Marta tried to cheer her up. "Belgium and Holland are getting closer to conquering France," she continued. "Americans have climbed the Alps into Italy and Russia is moving toward Slovakia. The German army is being surrounded, and at this rate the war could be over before we know it."

"Where do these rumours come from?" asked Clara skeptically. "Why are we supposed to believe anything we hear these days?"

"Look, I'm not saying everything we're hearing is true. But there are too many positive reports to ignore. Some recent inmates have been able to smuggle in radios, so news like this is being heard on an almost daily basis."

"Well, I still don't believe it," Clara replied, looking down at the ground. After everything that had happened, Clara couldn't trust these reports.

"Clara, look around you. People are smiling more these days. They actually look happy. They can sense that things are changing. You have to feel it, too."

"Talk to me when the walls come down and we're allowed to walk out of here. I'll start smiling when those guards over there aren't pointing guns in my face."

Clara had now been imprisoned in Terezin for a year and a half. And in that time, she had lost so much that was precious to her. Would life ever be the same? In spite of herself, she still wondered what it would be like to walk out of Terezin. Clara pictured herself returning to her home, where she dreamed that her bedroom would be waiting for her, untouched by the time that had passed. What would it feel like to sleep in a clean bed, to eat as much food as she wanted, and to live with her mother and father again? Maybe Marta was right. Perhaps there was still hope for a future. The possibility of freedom suddenly felt more real. Terezin was a constant roller-coaster ride, good and bad, hope and horror, triumph and tragedy. One minute you were up and in the next you were plunged into despair.

Meanwhile, there were more and more transports heading to the east. Some said the Nazis were trying to clear out the ghetto, to remove the evidence that it had existed. Whatever the reason, each week, thousands of inmates were being called to the Hamburg barracks, where all those being deported were ordered to appear. Carrying a small suitcase containing a handful of belongings, they left on trains for the dreaded destinations to the east. When the orders for deportation were announced, inmates held their breath, praying not to be among those summoned to leave.

One day, Hanna's name was on the list, and she was ordered to report to the Hamburg barracks where she would join the next transport leaving Terezin.

"You have to appeal it, Hanna. You can apply for a request to have your deportation order postponed. I know you can. Remember, Monica's family did the same thing a few months ago and it worked. They haven't received new orders." Clara sat with her friend in the courtyard of the dormitory, sickened by the news and refusing to accept it.

"That was a long time ago, Clara," replied Hanna. "Besides, Monica's father was some kind of important leader in Prague. But the orders are different now. Pardons were possible back then, but not any longer. Anyone who receives an order to go, must go. That's just the way it is."

"When are you to leave?" asked Clara, her head lowered, staring at the pavement.

"Two days from now," replied Hanna. "Not much time to get ready. Then again," she said with a laugh, "there's not much to pack, is there?"

"Maybe it won't be so bad where you're going," whispered Clara. Her comment hung heavily in the air.

Clara wanted to scream and cry but she couldn't show

her friend how scared she really was. Why had Hanna been selected to go while Clara had not? What made Clara special? She thought back to her conversation with Jacob when he had asked her if she believed in fate. Was it just that Clara was lucky?

The next day, Clara sat and watched Hanna get ready. In front of her, Clara tried to stay calm. Hanna seemed positive and almost upbeat. It was almost as if she were trying to comfort Clara by being strong herself.

"Stop looking so depressed, Clara," Hanna said as she folded her clothes into her suitcase. Clara remembered the day they had arrived together and had lugged this same suitcase up to the top bunk of this room. They had slept next to each other for the past year and a half.

"I will look for you when this war is over. And I believe it's going to be sooner than we both think." Hanna's sudden confidence was amazing. Clara wondered whether she could be so calm, if she were in Hanna's shoes.

"At least I'm going with my parents," Hanna continued. "Do you remember when Eva's grandparents were ordered to go without the rest of her family? Now that would be worse than anything." Hanna dug under her mattress as she talked and finally pulled out a crystal stone.

"Here," she said, pulling Clara's arm toward her and placing the stone in the palm of Clara's hand. "I brought this with me when I came to Terezin and somehow the guards never found it in my suitcase. It's only a small rock but I've always loved its colour and always thought of it as a good-luck piece. I want you to have it."

The stone was an ordinary piece of quartz, the kind Clara would have found in any field back home. But it had been polished and buffed. It shone with a faint pink glow that bounced off the ceiling of the room. Clara was so touched that for a moment she couldn't speak.

"Hanna," she finally said, "you have to keep this. It's beautiful, but I can't accept it. I mean, you need luck for wherever you're going."

"No," replied Hanna firmly. "It's for you. Take it and when we see each other again, you'll show me that you've kept it safe."

Clara hugged Hanna tightly, blinking back the hot tears that threatened to spill from her eyes.

The two girls sat up well into the night, talking softly. It was important to spend as much time together as they could, to hold on to these last moments and store them up to use as fuel for the future.

Chapter Twenty-six

GOODBYE TO HANNA

MORNING CAME ALL TOO QUICKLY, and with it, the time for Hanna to leave. The day was grey and overcast. Cool raindrops fell on the ghetto, leaving puddles on the streets. The dreariness of the day matched the anguish in Clara's heart, as she walked with her friend toward the train station.

Mama had warned Clara not to go with Hanna to the depot. It was too dangerous. Stragglers in the vicinity of the trains could be grabbed by guards and shoved on board the departing transports at the last minute. But this time, Clara disobeyed her parents. Nothing was going to keep her away. If Hanna was going to face deportation, then the least Clara could do was be there at her side. Raindrops rolled down Clara's face, hiding the real tears that flowed from her eyes. She was silent and grim, while Hanna chattered away.

"At least the rain will keep the boxcars cool. Remember how hot it was inside the train when we first came here? In Terezin, I never know what's worse, the heat or the cold. Personally I think being cold is worse. When my feet get cold, nothing can warm me up. And then my whole body feels cold, and I'm so miserable."

On and on she rambled. Her words were like the rain-drops themselves, streaming out of her in an endless downpour. Clara shuddered in the cold as they neared the train station and saw the crowd of people already assembled there.

Hanna quickly moved ahead to join her family. Strangely, there was little tension in the air. It was almost as if the crowd had accepted the fact that they were leaving and that being anxious would only make the situation worse. Or perhaps the grown-ups were all just trying to be brave and calm for the children. Whatever the reason, it felt strange to Clara to see the long lines of people moving slowly and quietly toward the awaiting trains. Was she the only one who felt like screaming? Her heart pounded so loudly in her chest that she thought those around her would surely hear it. And yet, she too had to show a calm side. For the sake of her friend, Clara had to be brave.

She stood next to Hanna and her family, and moved forward with them, step by step as guards directed families toward the open boxcars. Finally Clara could delay no longer. It was time to say goodbye. She turned to Hanna and they fell into each other's arms, hugging tightly. Hanna had been Clara's sister, her soul mate, her confidante and her friend. They had shared so many difficult moments in Terezin, and wonderful moments as well. They had cried together and laughed whenever they could. Clara wanted desperately to tell Hanna that everything would be alright.

But she couldn't.

"Goodbye, Hanna. I'll miss you more than you can imagine."

"I hope you get a nice roommate to take my place in the dorm."

"No one will ever take your place. I've saved some bread for you." Clara forced the slices into Hanna's hands as the ghetto guards moved between them to push the families forward. Hanna turned several times to wave. Clara shoved ahead, trying to get a spot close to the ropes at the edge of the station. For a moment, she lost sight of her friend and she frantically searched the boxcars with her eyes, desperate to catch one last glimpse of Hanna. Then suddenly, she saw her again, at the window in front of her. Hanna continued to wave and shout Clara's name, while Clara could only stand and stare.

The train wasted no time in leaving. It slowly puffed and whistled its way out of the station while Clara stood there, waving. Be strong, she thought. Be brave, and pray each day that we will see each other again, as I will pray for you. Clara stood with her hand above her head until the last cloud of engine smoke had disappeared from the sky.

Chapter Twenty-seven

A NEW BEGINNING

"Excuse me, is this room number six?" A small voice interrupted Clara's thoughts and she looked down from her bunk to see a girl of about her age at the door of the dormitory. Clara nodded.

"I'm new here. The train just arrived and I was told to go to room number six. My parents have gone somewhere else. I'm not sure where." The girl bit her trembling lower lip, trying hard not to cry. Her expression was very familiar to Clara.

"Don't worry," said Clara. "I'm sure they're fine. They'll be assigned to a room somewhere else, but you'll probably be able to see them later. You're in the right place. My name is Clara."

"I'm Margaret," the girl replied, obviously relieved at the news of her family. "Everything is so scary here and I'm not sure what I'm supposed to do."

Slowly, Clara climbed down from the bunk and approached the new girl. "Well, Margaret, the first thing you have to do is find a bed and unpack your stuff. There's an empty cot next to mine. If you want, I'll help you put your things up there."

Margaret smiled and gratefully shook Clara's outstretched hand. "Oh, thank you. I'd love your help." Together they pulled the case up the ladder and onto the bed that had belonged to Hanna.

Clara talked to Margaret about the ghetto and its rules. She told her about the food lines, the curfews and about how to avoid the guards who were dangerous. She warned Margaret about the cold and the heat and the bugs. She also told her about the teachers and the other girls in the room. On and on Clara talked, knowing that in some small way, she was helping the new girl get settled, just as Jacob had helped Clara the day she first arrived. Clara didn't tell Margaret about the transports. She would learn about them soon enough. There was no reason to frighten her more right now.

"Margaret, do you sing by any chance?" Clara asked.

"Oh, I love to sing," she replied and for a moment her face seemed to light up with memories. "I used to be in a girls' choir in Amsterdam."

"There's an opera that we're doing here called 'Brundibar.' And I happen to know that there are a couple of openings in it. If you want, you can come with me this evening to audition."

"An opera! You mean a real performance? Here? But, how's that possible?"

For a moment Clara couldn't answer. How could she

explain to Margaret that in the midst of the horrors of the ghetto there could also be some happiness. "Brundibar" had given her hope and had helped ease her fears. If only for short periods of time, it had helped her rise above the hunger, loneliness and despair. Hanna and Jacob had also known how real and inspiring it had been. But now they were gone, and so was Peter, leaving a painful ache in Clara's heart. Still, she knew that no matter what the future might hold, she had to continue to find courage in the things around her, like new friends.

Clara rubbed a small pink crystal in her hand as she replied to Margaret. "Oh, you'd be amazed at what's possible — even in Terezin."

THE END

Epilogue

ON MAY 8, 1945, Russian tanks rolled through the streets of Terezin signalling the end of the war and the defeat of the Nazis. The handful of Jewish prisoners still alive in the ghetto crept cautiously from their rooms, afraid to believe that they were free. But soon they joined in cheering and waving as they realized that they had survived the war. Among them were Clara and her parents.

Clara had almost stopped hoping that this day might come. Even though the news filtering into the ghetto clearly showed that the Nazis were being conquered, it hardly mattered day to day. Transports had continued to leave for the east, with greater numbers of Jews on board. And thankful as she was that her name was not on the lists for deportation, Clara wondered why she and her parents were being spared. Her heart could not stop hurting. It ached for Peter and Jacob and Hanna and all the others who had died or been sent east. The day the Russian tanks entered Terezin was a day that was as painful as it was joyful for Clara.

It took several weeks before the inmates could organize transportation back to their hometowns. Clara and her parents finally found a truck that was going to Prague. So they too left and travelled back home to begin to pick up the pieces of their lives.

Clara was now fifteen. She had been a prisoner in Terezin for two years and two months. Her family's apartment was gone, taken over by a Czech family who had moved in and claimed all of the belongings that Clara's family had left behind. So the first order of business was to find a new place to live. An organization working with returning Jewish families managed to find them a flat. Papa found a job in one of the hospitals and mama got a job in the library. Clara returned to school and realized that, thanks to the teachers who had been in Terezin, she was hardly behind in any of her subjects.

The search for friends and relatives was of equal importance. Every day hundreds of notes were posted on the bulletin boards of every office building in town. The notes asked whether anyone had seen this person or knew the fate of that family. Even the Russian tanks in the centre of town were plastered with messages.

Each day after school, Clara made the rounds of these buildings, leaving her own notes and reading the notices on each wall. Over the next few weeks, her family was happily reunited with several cousins and friends. But with each joyous reunion there was also the tragic news of more deaths. One day, Clara read a response to one of her messages, which said that Hanna and her family had last been seen at a concentration camp called Auschwitz. There they had all died along with hundreds of thousands of other Jewish families. Clara cried for days after receiving this news.

One day, several weeks after she had returned to Prague, Clara approached the old synagogue next to the park where she had spent so much of her childhood. The synagogue was boarded up, and in terrible shape. Its walls too were covered in messages, desperate notes begging for information. Sighing deeply, Clara began to read through the newer ones. She was almost unaware of what she was reading when suddenly one message seemed to pop out at her. She grabbed the paper and read it with trembling hands. Quickly she dug into her bag for a piece of paper and a pencil. Her hands were still shaking as she quickly scribbled a reply and pinned it to the wall. Then, she turned and walked away, a brighter bounce to her step. Looking down at the piece of paper in her hand, she read again:

"A policeman has returned to Prague and is looking for a sparrow."

Author's Note

WHILE MOST of the characters in *Clara's War* are fictitious, the story is set in an accurate historical place and time. It is based on real events.

Terezin was a real place and during the Second World War operated as a concentration camp. Here, the Jews of Czechoslovakia were temporarily housed before being deported east to death camps. Today, Terezin is once again a pleasant town. Since 1991, a museum has been created in the building that was once the boys' dormitory.

The ghetto was run on a day-to-day basis by a committee, the Council of Jewish Elders. Jakob Edelstein was one of the leaders of that council. The committee was controlled by Czech guards who patrolled the ghetto and ran it under Nazi command. One of the cruellest Nazi officers in Terezin was Rudolf Heindl, who I have included as a guard in the story. He was known for his brutality to Jewish inmates.

Children in Terezin were separated from their parents; however, the process of assigning separate dormitories was lengthier than the process I describe in my story. In reality, children under twelve years of age initially stayed with their mothers, while fathers were assigned to separate barracks. It was only after one to two weeks that children were moved, first into rooms apart from their parents, and then into separate dorms. Likewise, it took some time for jobs to be assigned to the adults. It is unlikely that a woman like

Clara's mother would have been assigned to work in the kitchen so quickly. Working in the food line was a desirable position, as it was a place from which extra portions could be distributed, if one was careful.

Escapes from the ghetto were almost unheard of, although a few successful escapes did occur. Those who tried and were caught were publicly hanged or shot. In November, 1943, following one such attempted escape, there was a forced march out of the ghetto to a nearby field in order to count the inmates of Terezin. Many people died from cold or exhaustion or from being trampled in the rush back to the ghetto. The chronology in this story places this event at a later date.

The children of Terezin were secretly taught by their house leaders and by well-known artists, mathematicians and historians. After the war, a collection of children's drawings, paintings and poems, which had been hidden in Terezin, was discovered. Pieces of the collection can be seen today in museums in Israel, the Czech Republic and the United States. Friedl Dicker-Brandeis was one of the more famous artists and teachers. She was sent to Terezin in December, 1942 and felt it was her mission to help the children cope with the chaos of the ghetto by providing them with a form of artistic expression.

A secret magazine called *Vedem*, published by the older boys of the boys' dormitory, was another form of artistic expression. One copy of the magazine was hand-written weekly for over two years and read aloud at house meetings.

The magazine contained poetry, observations of life in the ghetto, essays and art. There were regular reviews of cultural programs including a review of "Brundibar," the opera that was performed by children in the ghetto.

During the Second World War, the Terezin ghetto did become a temporary home for some of Czechoslovakia's greatest artists, musicians and performers. Hans Krasa, the composer of "Brundibar," was an inmate in Terezin during this time, along with Rudolf Freudenfeld, who directed the opera and conducted the orchestra and Frantisek Zelenka, who designed the sets. Honza Treichlinger, a fourteen-year-old boy in Terezin, was cast as the first organ grinder. He became somewhat of a minor celebrity in the camp. He, along with most of the other actors and musicians, were eventually deported to concentration camps in the east where they were killed.

The opera was performed fifty-five times in Terezin and was profiled during an International Red Cross inspection. Karl Rahm was the Nazi commander of Terezin at the time of the Red Cross visit. During the inspection the Germans did everything possible to improve the look of the camp. They planted grass and flowers, brought in food and new clothing for the inmates, hid the sick and elderly and staged elaborate musical productions. There is a documented story that one of the inspectors approached a Jewish woman during the tour to ask her about conditions in the ghetto. She did in fact roll her eyes, hoping the visitors would ask more questions, but no one ever did. As soon as the inspectors left, the camp was returned to its previous state, and thousands of inmates were immediately deported to Auschwitz. Auschwitz was the destination of most inmates of Terezin — the most notorious of all concentration camps, where Jews by the hundreds of thousands were systematically put to death.

With the exception of the individuals noted above, the characters in *Clara's War* are fictitious. I have drawn from several sources and conversations with people who were children in Terezin at that time. One such person is John Freund, who is a survivor of Terezin and subsequently Auschwitz. John was a young boy of about twelve years of age when he was sent to Terezin. Although he himself never performed in "Brundibar," he did see several performances take place. He was friends with many of the children who were in the opera. Two of those people are still alive today: Ella Stein, who played the part of the cat; and Greta Hoffmeister, who was Aninka.

I first learned about the opera "Brundibar" when my daughter had the opportunity to perform in an English version of it. She played the part of the dog. It was remarkable to me that an opera so simple and yet so beautiful and significant could have been performed in the midst of the wretchedness and misery of the Terezin ghetto. It was also remarkable to learn that, as children were deported on to death camps, other children were recruited from the ghetto to take their place in the opera. The opera continued to survive in the ghetto, as it has endured to this day.

MAP OF TEREZIN

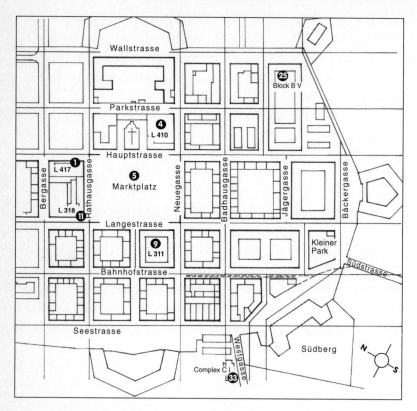

EXPLANATORY NOTES:

On the map, the names are in the original German. Many of the names end with the word "strasse," which means "street." The word "Marktplatz" means "Market place" or "Market square."

1. The Ghetto Museum. The former school of Terezin served as a boys' home.
4. Girls' home. This is where painting lessons were given by Friedl Dicker-Brandeis.
5. The square was fenced and inaccessible for prisoners. During the "embellishing campaign," it was adapted to a park and made free to use.
9. Sappers' barracks became a home for the aged prisoners and an auxiliary hospital.
11. Home for young and pre-school children. Terezin kindergarten.
25. Magdeburg barracks — a seat of the Council of Elders and the Jewish administration.
33. Sokol gymnasium. In the beginning, it was used as one of the hospital wards.

Transport arriving in Terezin
Negative no.: 24758
Photoarchive, Jewish Museum in Prague

Helga Weissová
Draw what you see.
Standing in the queue in front of the kitchen
For every meal – three times a day – one stood in an endless line
1942 pen and ink drawing and watercolours

Out of 15,000 children brought to Theresienstadt and later deported
to Auschwitz, only 132 survived the Holocaust. Helga Weissová was
one of them. She was 13 years old when she painted this image.

From: Helga Weissová. Zeichne, was Du siehst: Zeichnungen eines Kindes
aus Theresienstadt/Terezin = Maluj, co vidis = Draw what you see, ed. by
Niedersächsiesche Verein zur Förderung von Theresienstadt/Terezin e. V.
Wallstein Verlag Göttingen, 1998.

Replica of a children's barracks
photo credit: Sarah Silberstein Swartz

Poster advertising Brundibar
photo credit: Sarah Silberstein Swartz

Original ticket stub
for a performance of Brundibar

Performance of Brundibar
Chorus Scene
Terezin, 1944
Photoarchive, Jewish Museum in Prague

Hans Krása
Composer of Brundibar
Negative no.: 24.951
Photoarchive, Jewish Museum in Prague

AGMV Marquis

MEMBER OF SCABRINI MEDIA

Quebec, Canada
2001